THE CARPET
OF BONES

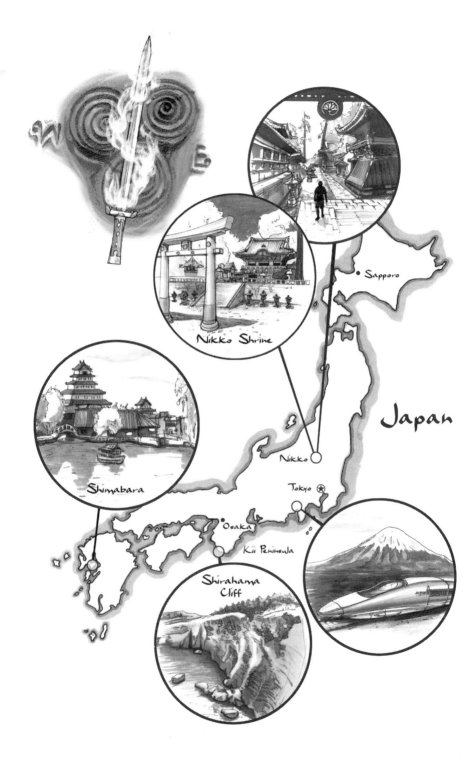

Sapporo

Japan

Nikko Shrine

Shimabara

Nikko

Tokyo

Osaka

Kii Peninsula

Shirahama Cliff

THE CARPET OF BONES

Lena Wood

❋❋❋❋❋❋❋❋❋❋

Standard
PUBLISHING
Bringing The Word to Life®

Text © 2006 Lena Wood.
© 2006 Standard Publishing, Cincinnati, Ohio. A division of Standex
International Corporation. All rights reserved. Printed in USA.
Project editor: Lindsay Black
Content editor: Amy Beveridge
Copy editor: Lynn Lusby Pratt
Cover and interior design: Robert Glover
Cover oil paintings: Lena Wood
Map illustration: Daniel Armstrong
Scripture taken from the HOLY BIBLE, NEW INTERNATIONAL
VERSION®. NIV®. Copyright © 1973, 1978, 1984 by International
Bible Society. Used by permission of Zondervan. All rights reserved.

Library of Congress Cataloging-in-Publication Data

Wood, Lena, 1950-
    The carpet of bones / Lena Wood.
       p. cm. — (Elijah Creek & the armor of God; #7)
    Summary: Elijah and his clan travel to Japan, where they learn about a secret
network of allies as well as an ancient enemy called Lotus, and along the way
they discover what may be the last piece of armor for their mission of spiritual
warfare.
    ISBN 0-7847-1535-1 (pbk.)
    1. Christian life—Fiction. 2. Friendship—Fiction. 3. Japan—Fiction.]
I. Title. II. Series: Wood, Lena, 1950- Elijah Creek & the armor of God; bk. 7.
    PZ7.W84973Car 2006
    [Fic] —dc22

                                                        2006011689

                    ISBN 0-7847-1535-1

    02 01 00 09 08 07 06   9 8 7 6 5 4 3 2 1

to **Hinsons,
Huddlestons, Turners . . .**
all those who do battle at the gates

Deepest appreciation to:
Dawn *for the dream*

Haruka *for the help*

the **Takagakis** *and* **Suzukis** *and* **Mukaiyamas,**
our Japan connection

&
The Sword Bearer

The grass withers and the flowers fall, but the word of our God stands forever.

—Isaiah 40:8

Chapter 1

IT was too quiet. The coming of spring marked more than a year since I'd made it out of Gilead, the isolated gorge in Telanoo where I'd nearly frozen my foot off and died of thirst. I'd also survived Abner's Latin class, a slower way of dying, stretched out over two whole semesters.

Reece's mom and Officer Taylor had gotten married. (A week before the ceremony, Reece's dad came back and hung around acting weird, but the whole police force was at the wedding, so there wasn't any trouble.) We four—Reece, Rob, Marcus, and myself—were all in various stages of driver's ed, constant reminders of Mei being gone. She was in Japan where getting a license costs thousands.

And I was back on the track team—Mom insisted. I had laid low for months, saying that I needed to give my foot time to heal, but I was more concerned with protecting the priceless Tear of Blood diamond by staying out of the limelight. After rejoining the team, my picture was in *The Magdeline Messenger* once for winning regionals, but I was just a big blur crossing the finish line, so that was good. Since nothing sinister had happened over the last year, I figured anyone hunting for the diamond had lost my scent. But just to be safe, my shadow rarely ever darkened Main Street in Magdeline, Ohio. If I had to go into town,

I'd cut through Owl Woods, dodge Morgan's prize bulls,
cross the tracks, and wind through back streets. Not that I
was afraid. After Gilead, I couldn't think of one thing that
scared me: not hunger or cold or nests of blue racers. Not
even the voice of the evil one—which also had gone quiet.
The whole Gilead nightmare had pretty much cleaned the
cobwebs from every dark corner of my mind. Now, I don't
recommend lying facedown under a two-ton stone slab
in the dead of winter for any reason, but Reece said God
worked it out for good. She called the fearlessness in me the
work of the Holy Spirit. I didn't understand it, but I didn't
doubt it. Reece had always known more about God than I
did.

My clan of four got together every now and then to do
Bible studies, which were sometimes interesting. But as far
as the search for the sword was concerned? Zero. God wasn't
giving any new clues. Mostly we went about life like regular
kids while the belt of truth, breastplate of righteousness,
shoes of peace, shield of faith, helmet of salvation, and right
arm of fellowship hung on a mannequin collecting dust
in the attic of The Castle. Sometimes I'd go up there and
sit for hours in the dim light, just looking at the armor,
wondering if this was how Dowland ended up crazy. But no,
the waiting hadn't done him in; greed had. He'd really been
searching for the Tear of Blood all along and never found
it. For sure, Dowland would have rolled over in his grave to
know his treasure had been in the helmet the whole time

and was now in the sweaty palm of the kid he'd tried to kill, a kid named George Telanoo. (Which was really me, Elijah Creek. But after the sales manager in New York Jewelers went into a fever over the diamond, I'd gone incognito as the geeky George from Georgia, stashing the Tear of Blood in ever-changing secret places—just in case.)

Over the year the clan got a few chatty notes from the Stallards, asking about our progress on the search for the sword. They'd moved to Boston and told me to put off sending them any of my blood until they got established.

Rob and Emily were getting to be a kind of thing, though Rob followed Marcus's advice about not getting too cozy with a nonbeliever. Reece and I were still best friends and then some. She kept feeling that God was telling us to go to Japan and help Mei, but nobody had that kind of money except Marcus. Meanwhile, the armor sat in Rob's attic without its sword, a ragtag relic inscribed with words of power. Just standing there waiting . . .

Camp Mudjokivi geared up for another summer. And except for the crazy fact that Florence's was now the new cool hangout—thanks to Marcus's addiction to grits and bacon—everything was the same old same-old.

I often wondered why we'd never found a left arm piece. Could it be a sign? Had God bared his arm for battle? Sometimes I'd imagine him waiting like an archer, his eye on a target, elbow locked, and I was the arrow drawn into the bow he was pulling back . . . back . . . ever so slowly.

An arrow never knows when the archer is going to release the bowstring and send it flying. I can tell you from my experiences with bow hunting that when you get a target in sight, it's best to stay in smooth constant motion from the second you draw until the second you release. It was making me crazy, my life moving slow and fluid like an arrow aimed and circling the target but going nowhere. So imagine my surprise when one morning in early June I heard a knock on the door and opened it to find the Stallards standing there.

They were dressed in tropical shirts, white pants, and sandals with white socks. (I guess compared to Boston, June in Ohio felt like the tropics.) Dr. Dale had his usual shabby briefcase. Dr. Eloise said, "We tried to call several times on our way down, but the line was always busy."

"My sisters live on the phone now," I apologized. "Um, come in."

"Is your mother home?" Dr. Eloise asked skittishly.

"Yeah, she's reading out on the patio."

"Might we speak with her a moment?"

When Mom came in, she was shocked and seemed embarrassed—probably because of the negative way she'd talked about the Stallards during the past year. But she sat the old archaeologists on the sofa in the living room and offered iced tea. "I'll have to make some."

While she clattered dishes in the kitchen, I sat on the ottoman and whispered, "What's up?"

Dr. Eloise beamed, "Everything, Elijah! Everything's up!"

"Is that . . . good?"

She spread her hands out. "Who knows?" She leaned in suddenly. "The armor's still in your possession? The gem?"

"Yeah. But no sword."

"We have much news. Are the others available?"

"Rob's at acting camp, but he'll be back tonight."

"We have many things on our agenda: a peek at Gilead if you are agreeable to guiding us there, a discussion about The Window, and—at long last—details on the global conference! We've arranged for it to be held in Japan so that you and your friends may kill two birds with one stone."

"Actually three birds killed, my dear," said Dr. Dale. "Visiting Mei. The training. And the first battle."

"Okay, but we don't have the sword," I said, keeping my voice low. "Doesn't each piece have a lesson for us? Should we do a battle without our weap—"

She dismissed me with a wave of her fingers. "We've done our best; mustn't worry; have to move ahead."

Mom came back but stayed in the doorway as if she were afraid to get too close to the Stallards. "Tea's brewing." She paused awkwardly. "How can I help you?"

Dr. Dale said, "Perhaps your son told you that we requested a sample of his blood a while back, to help you trace your family roots."

Mom's jaw dropped. Her eyes drilled me. "No. He didn't."

Dr. Dale went on calmly, "Well, it's been . . . has it been

a year already? And we've been very busy—relocating. We have substantial resources at our disposal and have taken the liberty to check into the MacMerrit family line. Your genetic information will help greatly. But that is only one reason for our visit. I'm sure you know how badly the children have wanted to reunite with their friend Mei Aizawa."

Mom smiled blankly.

"We can be of help there as well. Our global conference is in August and takes place in the mountains north of Tokyo. Our associates were glad to adjust their plans—change the date and the location—for that very purpose. We apologize that it has taken us so long, but the conference involves many people spread out over sixty countries."

Having known the Stallards for more than two years now, I still had to snicker at their nerve. Even talking bloodletting and global meetings, how could Mom refuse? They'd gone to a bucket of trouble. She'd look like the jerk of the century.

Mom tried to smile. "Well, I certainly appreciate all the work you've done, but—"

"Yes, yes! The money," Dr. Eloise cut in, rocking back dramatically. "The money! Always a problem in this world." Then she chirped, "But! We can be of help there too. Our constituents—though their resources are slimmer than you would imagine—are chipping in. Granted, it won't cover the whole cost, but think of the financial perks: for three weeks you won't have to feed the boy!" The Stallards chuckled and winked at me. "And what an opportunity for the children's education. By happy coincidence, a team of young people known as the Students of the Seven Seas will be at the conference. High school age, like Elijah."

She pulled out a pamphlet with a cruise ship on the front and handed it to Mom. Sounding like an encyclopedia salesman, Dr. Eloise gave her spiel: "Your child will have the chance to discover the world through others' eyes and experience fascinating cultures. And look there on page three: information about the conference. As a mother myself, I'd jump at the chance to give my child a visit to the lush mountains and teeming cities of Japan for a fraction of the regular exchange program cost. A real bargain."

Mom frowned at the pamphlet. The short leash she'd had me on for the last year was straining, ready to snap. I wanted to go! I could practically smell the salt air. I could taste the fancy little Japanese meals Mei made when we built the road through Telanoo. I could hear Marcus's running travelogue and Rob's smart remarks. I could see Reece at my side grinning from ear to ear.

"Russ and I will need to discuss this," Mom said doubtfully.

I scooted to the edge of the ottoman. "It's educational, Mom! For social studies this fall, I could do a paper on Japanese government or something!"

The Stallards smiled at me, their eyes glittering in a way that was always a little unnerving. Dr. Eloise stood. "Of

course, Jodi. Of course, talk it over with your husband.
We're in the area for a few days on several items of
business." She turned to me. "While we're here, Elijah, we'd
love to see the place where you nearly lost your life."

I went straight to Dad, spilling everything before Mom
could talk him out of it. "It's three weeks at the end of
summer, Dad. I can line up a replacement for my chores.
And about them drawing my blood, okay, sure it's weird,
but the Stallards know how to find things out. They tracked
down Francine Dowland when the police couldn't! It might
help Mom to know the truth about her past."

Somehow in the next few days, after a parent meeting
with the Stallards and a late-night phone conversation
with Dom Skidmore, my parents reluctantly gave the okay.
I thanked them a zillion times. Especially Dad, because
nowadays more than ever he depended on me to fill in the
gaps at camp and—as he'd say with a sad smile—"Keep
an extra eye on the twins, will you? Just until your mom is
back to her old self." I could tell he was going to miss me.

The camp nurse gave me a strange look about drawing
blood but went ahead. I'd done so much for her over the
years—calming kids down when they got sand thrown in
their eyes, carrying bigger kids up to her station when they
sprained an ankle—she owed me big time.

My blood got sent off to who-knows-where, and then I

took the clan and the Stallards—outfitted in safari shorts and mountain boots—to Gilead for archaeology and a picnic. We drove two carts through Telanoo until the road ended, then headed west, hiking the rough terrain. We guys took turns carrying Reece on our backs.

The little old scientists cooed over Gilead's wall inscribed in ancient *Ogham* script: "The right hand of God is a shield—a prayer." They took pictures and rubbings and insisted again that we keep my discovery quiet. I told the story of what happened there, and then we spread a picnic on the big slab of rock that had nearly killed me. Dr. Dale gave a prayer of celebration for my rescue, and we dove into the food.

Dr. Dale sat his skinny self on the ground cross-legged with his plate balanced on his knee, acting younger than he was, more spry. "You recall our telling you about The Window." On the ground in front of him, he spread a map of the world showing a wide strip of land above the equator, shaded in red. It reminded me of a map of Magdeline showing the path of damage after the tornado struck. "The Window encompasses almost sixty countries across ten thousand miles. To be sure, there are many dark and dangerous places in this sector, but millions of wonderful people and rich histories also. We choose to see it as a place through which the light can yet shine . . . until the clock ticks no more." As an afterthought he added, "We call it The Window, but it's also labeled the Zone of Despair or the

Belt of Terror by some international agencies." He gulped from his canteen. "And rightfully so."

We ate and stared at the map—they'd get to the point soon enough. They mentioned that in Japan we'd be "storming a stronghold" and attending a few classes for "training." We'd meet other young people from all over the world: the Students of the Seven Seas—the SOS for short.

Reece said, "I called Mei, and she's so excited! She wants us to come to her house and visit her church. I promised we would; is that okay? The Trentons are missionaries there. Their church is small, and the people have terrible problems: sickness, accidents, and mental illness. I feel so bad for her, so I thought we could talk to the people."

The Stallards exchanged knowing looks. Then Dr. Eloise gushed to Reece, "Your very presence will bless them! Certainly we will go and fellowship together!"

Dr. Dale slurped a bite of melon. "A prayer journey may be in order there. We'll check on the—" he hesitated, "the spiritual climate of the place."

They coached us on Japanese customs—a lot of which Reece already knew—like shoe manners. In Japan they have outdoor shoes, indoor slippers, porch slippers, and bathroom slippers, and you have to know when to switch out of one and into the other. The Japanese are all about being clean. We discussed the customs of gift-giving and obeying rules of courtesy. The Japanese people always seem to act courteously, with one exception: getting on a train at rush hour—in which case you run like a maniac, push your way in, don't get separated from your group, and try not to get trampled or stuck in the door.

The Stallards gave Rob the location names; he wanted to help plan the itinerary. They told Marcus privately (though I overheard it) to make sure Dom stayed in contact with the rest of the parents.

As we finished up, Rob—fresh from acting camp and buzzed about going to Japan—exploded into a karate-ninja act. He took off down the canyon, hand-chopping trees on the way. He threw himself shoulder-first onto the ground, rolled and spun in one motion into attack posture, and faced us. Wailing a bunch of nasal, high-pitched vowels as a war cry, he came at us full tilt and took a flying leap at the slab—for a spectacular stunt jump over the picnic.

He almost made it. His toe caught the edge of the slab. One knee went into the potato salad, one hand scraped rock, the other slushed through cantaloupe as he hollered, "Yeeaam sorrreeee!" Dr. Dale leaped to his feet to escape the flying food. I was sure he'd be mad, since he'd paid for it all. But with a napkin pressed to his mouth, Dr. Dale bent double and slapped his knee for a good minute, while Rob—like a roast pig at a luau—lay there in the middle of the feast: ninja à la carte.

Marcus and I dragged him off to the little waterfall at the end of the canyon. We each grabbed an arm and stretched him under the falls to clean him off. While he howled like a torture victim, Reece cackled and Marcus yelled, "No more acting camps for you, man! You are out of control!"

Nothing more was said about The Window and what it had to do with our trip to Japan. On the long hike out of Gilead, Dr. Eloise drew me aside. "Elijah, the Tear of Blood?"

"I still have it."

"No sign of trouble?"

"Not yet."

She nodded. "Very good. Keep our contact information with you at all times. And don't take any chances."

We walked for a while. "Dr. Eloise, is my life in danger?" She paused for a long time—which to me was not a good thing. I said, "This problem won't ever go away, will it?"

"If you mean people wanting the Tear of Blood, no, dear. It is perhaps the most prized gem of all." She walked on, huffing and puffing as we headed back toward the golf carts. I helped her across the dry creek bed, and she thanked me. "We have not heard any more from our contacts in the diamond industry since the first . . . information leak." Her tolerant smile was worse than getting chewed out.

"I'm really sorry about that," I said.

"Concealing your identity was a wise move. Treasure hunters are probably checking leads in Georgia, which is why we've heard nothing. But . . . ," her smile went thin, "the silence is a little unnerving. Perhaps it will be good for all of us to be out of the country, even for a short while."

Chapter 2

"**HOW** are everyone's preparations coming?" Reece asked.

We were into July, hanging out in the Tree House Village doing a Bible study and eating ice cream. The Stallards had driven off waving and saying, "*Mata atode!*" Then life had gone quiet again, the same old same-old.

I answered Reece's question with a question. "Your mom's making crafts for us to take as gifts, right? So I'm pretty much ready: clothes lined up, passport and Quella. I sold off a few more snakes, and I'm working overtime at camp."

She said, "But is everyone reading the Bible and praying?"

Rob added to my answer, "Elijah and I are mowing yards too, so the money's coming in."

She huffed. "I know about the money. The church will take up an offering, and the Stallards sent a big chunk. But they said we should do a prayer journey at Mei's town."

"So?" Rob asked. "Don't you pray once you get there?"

She went ballistic. "You haven't been *praying!?*"

"I pray!" he defended.

Reece shot a questioning look at Marcus, who shrugged confidently, "We're in the kingdom, baby. Chill."

I said, "The Stallards didn't say we had to do anything special, Reece."

She raged, "But for Heaven's sake, we have to be ready! Marcus, didn't your dad always train before he went on a mission? Didn't he know who the enemy was?" She turned to Rob. "And when you're starring in a show, don't you read the script first?" She turned to me. "Don't you get food, water, and a tent before you go into the wild?"

Marcus said coolly, "Preach on, sista!"

I couldn't tell if she was hyper about seeing Mei and helping her church, or nervous about her bone condition, or what. She was down to using a cane, but anything could aggravate it. I didn't want her getting upset. I said calmly, "We'll be staying in hotels and stuff. We won't need tents."

"I mean preparation for the *prayer journey!*"

Grunting in frustration, I muttered, "I've done prayer walks, Reece. It's the same thing . . . isn't it?"

Marcus was now in a mood. "I travel all the time, Elliston. A lot more than you."

"I don't mean the traveling part!" she snipped.

"Calm down, everybody," Rob said.

"We're in trouble, guys," Reece said dramatically. "I'm calling the Stallards."

Reece made good on her threat, and in a week we had a letter back marked "URGENT."

Children—Since ours is a spiritual journey as well as an international one, you must prepare on both levels. Perhaps we were remiss in not discussing this in detail. Take passports, lightweight clothes, and comfortable shoes, of course; travel light. But do please read your Scriptures and pray! Refer to Luke 9 where you will see that a change of clothes and pocket money are not so important as having God's power and your own testimony. Since we are not privy to the particulars of the adversary in the second stronghold we'll visit—on the Kii Peninsula where Mei lives—it might be wise to fast, perhaps once a week; let your heart lead, and do not go to extremes. The point is to make special time for the Word and prayer.

Perhaps we assumed too much, children. Do you even want to participate in storming a stronghold? Are you at all aware of the religion and culture of this country? Do you not believe in the power of prayer? If not, this trip could do more harm than good. Please talk this over among yourselves and reply immediately. There is still time to get a refund on the flight tickets.

In his service, The Stallards

With less than a month to go, we were suddenly cramming for finals. Practically overnight, Rob became an expert on Japan. I happened by the library one day to find him behind a stack of books. He perked up when he saw me. "Hey, Elijah, I've made a map of our itinerary: two days to get there because we lose a day over the international date line. Osaka to Nikko, a week at the conference, then to Kii Peninsula for five days. A day to get to Shimabara. The Stallards want to show us some archaeology there. Then car ferry to Osaka. We're going to be all over Japan!"

"Cool." I sat down and waved at Mrs. Otto, who was peering down the aisle at us.

"Hot, actually," said Rob. "The average temperature for August is eighty degrees; the average rainfall six inches. Possible typhoons. We should take clothes that dry fast."

"One backpack and a carry-on," I reminded him.

"Right. Here's what I know about the religion." He shoved a big picture book at me. "Those little oriental house-looking things are Shinto shrines. And this is a *torii,* a gateway to the gods. You always go through a *torii* to get to a shrine. It's mostly nature worship. Everything— even rocks and trees—has a *kami*, or a god, inside it. But people can be worshiped too." He shoved another book at me with pictures of big golden gods. "The other religion is Buddhism, following a man who lived around 500 BC. I skimmed several books, and I'm confused. It's about reincarnation and getting to nirvana, which means nonexistence. There's also ancestor worship—"

I interrupted him to show off what little I knew, "Which is why Mei used to pray to her grandmother."

"Yeah. Hey, are you taking your diamond?"

"It's not mine, and I don't know."

"My people!" Marcus appeared and slid into a seat beside me. He spotted the books on Buddhism. "I've known that stuff since my trip to Thailand when I was nine!"

"Shhhhhhhhhhhh!" Mrs. Otto went off like a steam train.

"There are a bunch of different kinds," Rob whispered authoritatively.

"It's all worshiping people and statues," Marcus said.

"Fear of spirits and demons. Idols. The same as where my ancestors come from in Africa." He leaned back with his hands knotted behind his head.

"We've heard about your voodoo a million times," Rob snipped. "Find something else to brag about."

Two weeks before we left, I was dashing out of the hardware store on a crack-of-dawn camp errand when I nearly collided with a cup of coffee—carried by the New York Jewelers guy. Our eyes locked. And even though I was taller, better dressed, and with a shorter haircut than when I'd first shuffled into his store and naively plopped down the Tear of Blood, he recognized me.

Muttering, "Excuse me," I sidestepped him and moved on. My heart sank. I ducked into an alley, feeling his eyes drill into my back. I dashed across the town's back parking lot, jumped a hedge, and scooted down the bank to the tracks—just as the 7:05 barreled past. A blast of hot greasy air, the rumble of heavy wheels, and an ear-splitting whistle knocked me back. *Close call!* I covered my ears and waited. I crossed the fence to Morgan's farm and leaped over. My foot plopped down into a fresh, squishy cow pile. *Drat!*

I was dragging my foot through the grass to wipe off the stinking stuff when I heard a snort and a heavy thud behind me. *Oh no* . . . I knew without looking that it was one of Morgan's prize Angus bulls protecting his turf. Slowly I turned. The monstrous horned beast snorted, tossed his big black head angrily at me, and stomped the ground—his way of saying, "Get out!" My adrenaline kicked in, and before he could charge me, I went back over that fence, light as a fairy.

Trudging home along the tracks—the smell of hot grease and bull dung still in my nose, the sound of my feet crunching gravel, my veins still throbbing, and sweat collecting in my eyebrows—something in me snapped. It wasn't just the New York Jewelers guy or the train or Morgan's bull. It was the pressure of the "spiritual preparation" that I really didn't understand. It was Rob asking if I was going to take *my* diamond to Japan, me getting mad at him (when in fact I *had* formed a strong attachment to it). But I was tired of thinking up new hiding places for it, tired of wishing I could let Reece keep it to take the pressure off me (but afraid one of her nosy friends would find it). I was frustrated seeing Dad worried about money all the time while hidden in my room was a huge fortune in a bean-size rock. And another thing: the armor wasn't complete, yet we were supposed to "storm a stronghold." Without the sword of the Lord? What kind of sense did that make?

The icing on the cake was a cryptic note from the Stallards the day before, which ended with: *We realize this will sound silly, but our friend has had a recurring dream, and she is worried about our safety. In her dream there was a flower, a rather plain one, which had no fragrance or medicinal use. She knew—as one knows in dreams without understanding how—that if one moved the flower or looked at it too long, it would die. And the flower said, "Don't move me or try to change me!"*

Our friend senses danger for our journey and will not be comforted by our reassurances that Japan is perhaps the safest country in the world. Few Westerners understand this. The crime rate is low. The people are immaculately clean, so there is little chance of contracting a fatal disease. Public transportation is well maintained, the food is carefully prepared, and the water supply is rigorously tested. If this flower riddle makes sense to any of you, please tell us so we can assuage our friend's worries. And please pass the reassuring facts about Japan along to your parents. We are looking forward to a grand time!

That night I lay awake in bed. I held the red diamond to the light, watching its triangular facets sparkle. Shaped like a tear, the color of blood. *What am I supposed to do with you? Should I take you or leave you? Why do you exist in the first place? Why did someone centuries ago put you in the armor?*

It was priceless and useless at the same time. I couldn't sell it. But it was only a matter of time before someone would rob me or kill me to have it.

What if New York Jewelers connects me to Camp Mudj and hires hit men while I'm gone? Dad could get death threats and not even know why. My mom and sisters could be kidnapped. I pictured my family bound and gagged, jewel thieves ransacking the house while I was off in Osaka eating sushi, the gem stashed safely in my belly button and sealed with duct tape.

What had the Stallards said about its meaning? That

from the ancient legend of the Tear of Blood came the Hindu custom of painting a red dot in the forehead to show service and sacrifice. Rob had discovered that, in Eastern folklore, a red diamond symbolized a warrior. *It's in the helmet, so its purpose has to be related to salvation. Its message has to be more than "People want me, and they hate you for having me. They're out for your blood!"* I fell asleep with the gem in my hand and a prayer full of questions in my mind.

In the middle of the night, I woke up with a crazy idea. *It's insane. It's awful. It's great!* I sat up, found the stone under my pillow, and held it under my bedside lamp, deciding, *Whatever the others think about the Tear of Blood and what should be done with it doesn't matter. You're the one connected with it, Creek. It's your call. Not the clan. Not the Stallards. Not New York Jewelers. You answer to God about this and to no one else. After all, it is his armor, his tears, his blood.*

I was up the rest of the night sketching.

The next morning I showed up at Rob's in a shirt and tie and dress pants. "Your dad has a good camera, doesn't he?"

"Yeah," he answered. "What are you dressed up for?"

"Business. The camera has a macro lens?"

"Yeah."

We spent the next hour taking pictures of the stone.

"What's up?" Rob asked.

"Don't ask."

He scowled at me but went on helping with close-ups of

the diamond in the sun, where its fire shot right into your eyes. We got pictures of me holding it in my hand, placed next to a ruler to show its size, and so on.

"Thanks," I said, taking the film and the gem. I went to the drugstore, told the photo girl to rush the pictures through, not caring whether she looked at them or not. I was done with the cloak-and-dagger stuff. I got a chocolate shake—breakfast—and waited on the pictures. Then I crossed Main Street and strolled into New York Jewelers, reminding myself, *The Tear of Blood is not about money. It's about salvation.*

The sales manager was waiting on a young couple. I dallied near the door at a watch display. When he saw me he dropped the ring he was showing and called out, "I'll be right with you." Another five seconds and he had excused himself to come wait on me.

"Take your time," I nodded toward the couple and lost the Georgia accent I'd faked the last time. "I'll wait."

"Interested in watches today? We have—"

"Diamonds," I replied. "I'm interested in diamonds."

He went pale. In a minute he'd rushed the couple out.

I pulled the diamond out of my pocket and laid it on the counter. "You want a piece of the action? You got it. A piece, that is. I need this cut into six pieces."

He gasped in air so hard he choked on his spit.

I went on. "Cut it into six small stones. I keep five; you get one as payment. Here are the specifications." I pulled out the paper with my sketches on it and laid it on the counter. "I know what this is, sir. It's the Tear of Blood, the Netsach Prism. The only pure red diamond ever found."

"Y-y-you can't—" he stammered, horrified at my idea.

"I can, and I will. But hey, if you don't want a piece of the one and only Tear of Blood, that's your business."

I picked it up and held it in front of his face. His shoulders went stiff. His eyes glazed over.

In a stern voice I said, "My sources tell me you've created quite a stir in the global gem business. You spilled the beans." *Spilled beans*?! I yelled at myself. *You sound like a kid, Creek. Talk businesslike.* "Unwise, sir," I continued. "With such lack of discretion, you're lucky I'm not taking my business elsewhere."

"You don't know what you're doing! It's a world treasure!" he said desperately.

I leveled my eyes with his. "I know exactly what I'm doing. The cutting will proceed in my presence; the stone is never to be out of my sight. If you don't have the skill to do it, call in a master gem cutter. I need the project completed in two weeks. Not a day later."

He looked doubtfully at the sketches.

I waffled. *Bad idea, Creek. You've done it again. He's not going to go for it—there's not enough time. What's more, he sees you cleaned up and looking like your regular self. He's gotta know you're from around here. He knows you're not from Georgia. Cover's blown.* I snapped the stone, enclosing it into my fist. "Too bad." I headed for the door thinking, *From this moment on, I officially have no life. Every moment I'll be jumping at shadows, imagining that I'm being followed, wondering if my house is being ransacked. I'll have to leave Magdeline and never come back.*

"Mr. Telanoo?"

I'll stay in Japan longer . . . or move to Ireland and live at Murlough House and help out there . . . maybe the Stallards would put me up in Boston for a while.

"Mr. Telanoo?"

He's talking to me! I turned.

Ashen-faced and short of breath, he said, "I have a friend, best in the business. I'll get him here Thursday."

"Tomorrow."

"I don't know if—"

"I'm out of time." I acted like I was leaving.

"All right!" he barked.

"Good." I paused a minute at the open door, giving him the steeliest look I could muster, and said darkly, "Don't underestimate me."

I, George Telanoo, slipped into the back room of New York Jewelers every morning for the next two weeks, a few hours before the store opened. The salesman sent the regular guy on vacation. The master gem cutter shook like he had palsy when he saw the Tear of Blood and found out what I wanted him to do. Obviously, he'd agreed to do the work before he knew exactly what it was. I acted impatient and told him to get a grip or I was leaving. (I couldn't believe myself. But I just kept picturing how cool and brave the

Stallards were at facing down Cravens in Dublin when he discovered they were looking for the armor of God. That's the only way I faked my way through. That, and a lot of praying.)

Once the initial cut was made and the Tear of Blood lay in pieces, the gem cutter breathed a little easier. There was no turning back now. Day after day I sat close, watched his every move. He'd stop working occasionally, breathe deeply, and mutter words like, "Utterly magnificent . . . Lights and perfections! It's the core of the earth afire!"

They played innocent and tried to squeeze information out of me, but I'd say, "When we're done here, you'll have a piece of the Tear of Blood. You want more? You ain't gettin' more." *Drats.* I'd meant to use business lingo like *breach of confidence* and *the firm's acquisitions* and *my fiscal year is in ruins.* They probably didn't buy it for a minute, that I was a whiz kid wheeler-dealer named Telanoo. Didn't matter. They wanted their tiny hunk of the treasure.

Every day I'd take the diamond pieces and head home right before the store opened for the day. I'd wind through Magdeline's back streets and backyards until I knew I wasn't followed. Then I'd cut across the tracks, ever watchful for Morgan's bulls. I'd work late at camp to make up the time I lost in the morning. And in those two weeks I often wandered out to the porch in the middle of the night and listened for footsteps. Jewel thieves. In the tense silence I'd say in my heart, *El-Telan-Yah, I know you're there.*

I hardly slept.

Chapter 3

A week before takeoff, the clan got Bibles and water bottles and went up on Devil's Cranium for an official clan powwow. They knew nothing about what was happening with the Tear of Blood.

As I got the fire going, Reece said, "I've been studying Psalms because it's the *Warrior*. Here's my favorite verse: 'Lift up your heads, O you gates; be lifted up, you ancient doors, that the King of glory may come in. Who is this King of glory? The LORD strong and mighty, the LORD mighty in battle. . . . He is the King of glory.'"

"Gates . . . ," Rob said thoughtfully. He pulled out a notebook and showed her a picture of a *torii* at a shrine. "This is a gate of the gods."

She blew a gasket. "That's . . . that's it then . . . the gates! I get it—why those words kept jumping out at me. When I see a gate, I'm supposed to pray those verses!"

Everybody said they were pretty much ready. I didn't want to make a big deal about Reece's condition because she seemed okay. I sure didn't want a repeat of the nerve-wracking days before Ireland when her prospects of making it seemed slim to none. I knew how she could have a setback any minute. From listening to Rob and Marcus, I also knew how much walking we'd be doing. In Ireland we drove everywhere; In Japan it's all buses and trains and lots of steps. She was probably worried about it. So when the guys were busy on another conversation, I looked across the fire to her and said in a tough voice, "Same as always, Elliston. If I'm going, you're going."

"Sure, Creek," she smarted off, saluting me like Marcus does sometimes, "over and out."

Operation Tear of Blood was completed the day before takeoff. I walked out of New York Jewelers for the last time, looked back at the sales manager, and said, "You have what you wanted, or as much of it as you're going to get. The rest is my business. Any hint of trouble my way and the police will know where to look." I tapped the store's name emblazoned on the glass door, then swaggered down Main Street, proud of myself for what I'd done. Relieved. Excited. Sick to my stomach.

The Stallards came to stay at the Wingate Bed and Breakfast and Tea Room the night before takeoff. They'd brought a ready-to-assemble packing crate for the armor of God. My clan and I were a little surprised. "We're taking it?" I asked.

"Oh, the conference must see it!" Dr. Dale insisted, more excitable than usual. "It will be the highlight! But first, might we have tea with Jodi and Dorian to discuss genealogy? Could that be arranged immediately?"

In twenty minutes we were sitting around two little

tables in the tea room of The Castle. The Stallards complimented Aunt Grace's orange cake and raspberry tea, and then Dr. Dale began, "Jodi, Dorian, Rob, and Elijah, regarding your ancestry: genetic studies are making swift strides, so our conclusions might yet be subject to further refinement. But you are certainly an interesting mix of peoples. The MacMerrits can be traced back to Scotland where—and this is a striking point which will interest Elijah—Creek Indians were often taken, either voluntarily for the sake of getting an education, or by force as a curiosity for the Europeans. We've been able to sketch out the family line from Isabel's parents near the Isle of Magdeline—later named Seven Avon Place—back to the MacMerrits of Scotland, who intermarried with the Creeks."

"You mean I'm a Creek!?" I cried. "I really am Indian?"

"Me too?" Rob asked weakly.

"Genetics and old church records indicate as much. You, Elijah, are perhaps doubly so. We've checked out your father's lineage as well, though with fewer resources. It appears that Russ's ancestors were also some of those Native Americans taken to Europe in the 1700s, who returned to the Deep South generations later with the surname they'd been given: Creek."

"I'm twice an Indian?" I said in a happy fog.

"And heavily Scotch-Irish too."

Mom eyed them curiously. "Goodness, you went to a lot of trouble."

Glancing at me, Dr. Eloise admitted, "Our motives are not entirely pure; we are immensely curious about the boy." She cleared her throat and went on. "Jodi, we were only able to find that your real father's first name was Simon, and that he worked with the newspaper or a dairy farm, perhaps one and then the other. Your parents' marriage license was destroyed, but your mother Isabel has a younger cousin, a Portia Ridley, who is still living in Ennis, County Clare. She works at a children's bookstore. She has cut ties with your side of the family, but we spoke with her directly, and she is willing to talk to you. Here is her number as well as numbers of a few relatives elsewhere in Ireland."

Mom was bowled over. She took the information into her outstretched hands as if it were gold. "Thank you so much! Dorian and I have been trying to find . . . how did you . . . ?"

Dr. Eloise said humbly, "One advantage of old age is that people are inclined to believe you are helpless. So ask a few questions, look pained and pathetic, wring your hands. . . . Anyone with half a heart . . . !" She and Dr. Dale traded chuckles.

(It occurred to me then what dumb kids and old people have in common: we can get away with stuff. Full-blown adulthood with all its high expectations wasn't going to cut me any slack; and all of a sudden, I wasn't crazy about getting there. But at least I had senility to look forward to.)

"What about Dowland?" I asked.

"Stanford Dowland was a relative, yes," said Dr. Dale.

"We believe it was he who tried to rescue Isabel from that horrible church-run workhouse. Clearly he was not successful. We must give the poor man credit for his heroic effort."

Dr. Eloise looked around the tea room. "The politician who built this lovely house was one of a line of rescuers who stole or bought babies—sometimes at a high price—from the Isle of Magdeline in order to spare them a fate like Isabel's. He bequeathed his mission of mercy to others, who stashed copies of the paperwork in a secret room here in The Castle, the small space I believe Grace and Dorian found while remodeling."

She asked for more tea as if that were the end of it. Dr. Dale whispered, "The MacMerrits, dear."

"Ah yes." She cleared her throat and said diplomatically, "What a curious lot they were: rough and rugged, handsome and heartless. More than a few skeletons in their closets! They were known for occult practices and were greatly feared in their heyday." She shook her head. "We believe that they did, in fact, acquire the armor of God and hide it in Leap Castle, believing as their pagan forefathers that they could 'hide all the magics' from the followers of Jesus."

Dr. Dale said, "Foolish bravado led them into dark spiritual waters they were not prepared to navigate. Rare photos in Irish archives show the later descendants as stark, miserable, haunted individuals. They have all but faded from history." Grimly he added, "The lure of the evil one from the beginning is still an effective ploy, children. But to clutch at spiritual power apart from God will ultimately result in a downward spiral into Hell—as with Satan himself—with no chance of deliverance."

We ate cake. Mom and Uncle Dorian—not believers like us—gave each other looks. Their being brother and sister, I figured they had their own eye code and were talking things over.

Dr. Eloise broke the quietness. "Elijah, all of you, we have been able to trace the MacMerrit lineage much further back, much further, which you might find even more thrilling than the Indian connection. But that discussion will have to wait. We have last-minute packing to do. Jodi and Dorian, best wishes and blessings on you! And, Grace, a lovely dessert!"

Dr. Dale threw down a big tip.

We gathered in the attic. The Stallards put the crate together, all the while chattering to each other: "After all these years! . . . Speculations put to rest . . . What fun we shall have! . . . The skeptics and doubters brought to the light! . . . All revealed!"

When the crate was assembled and the bags of packing straw opened, Dr. Dale beamed at his wife romantically, "My dearest, dearest Eloise! We have done it!"

Reece grinned at me. The guys looked down at their shoes.

We wrapped the pieces of armor in linen. I checked the inside of the helmet, which I'd repaired to look like it did before I dug out the diamond.

Dr. Eloise asked me, "And the stone?"

"Packed. Safe," I said with a guilty lump in my gut.

She patted the helmet. "Excellent."

We couldn't get Rob out of ninja mode. With stiff poses and guttural sounds, he neck-chopped the attic mannequins and leaped from the couch, hacking at rafters. He kicked the air yelling, "Neen-jaaaa!"

Marcus shook his head, "Ninjas are masters of stealth, Wingate. Stealth. They don't go around screaming like banshees. You couldn't be stealthy if your life depended on it."

Rob stopped dead. "Can't be stealthy? *Me?*"

I'd seen that wide-eyed, fake innocent expression before: when we were kids and I double-dog-dared him. This trip was going to be interesting.

There was the traditional crying and hugs from our parents, including Officer Taylor this time. Mom drove us to the airport, tense and quiet. Once there, she waved us through the first gate until we got in a long line and signaled that we'd be there a while. She blew me a kiss and disappeared.

We piled our luggage around us, including the crate stamped "FRAGILE: Antiquities Research Center." I guarded it with a watchful eye because people in line kept looking at it. The Stallards weren't about to let it go into the cargo hold. They wanted it in a special closet in the cabin. One by one we put our backpacks on the conveyor belt and watched them go through security x-ray. Once everyone else was through, Marcus and I hauled the armor crate onto the belt and watched the x-ray screen, curious about what it would look like, wondering if the security people would question it. The shape of the helmet came into view. I watched the eyes of the security screener go on alert. He paused the conveyor belt for a few seconds. Next came the breastplate with the shoes, belt, and arm piece tucked inside. Suddenly he stopped the belt and came up off his chair . . . because on the x-ray screen, mixed in with all the other shapes, was the perfect outline of a sword blade.

Chapter 4

✖✖

"**PLEASE** step over here," the guard said severely to Marcus and me. Two security people hauled the crate to a side table. "Please open this," one ordered.

The Stallards, who'd gone through and were talking with Reece and Rob, saw the problem and came right over.

I turned my back to the guard and mouthed, "Blade."

Dr. Dale didn't understand.

The guard asked, "Whose crate is this?"

"Mine," Dr. Dale stepped in. "I'm from Antiquities Research Center. Is there a problem?"

"Please open the crate, sir," the man said again.

Dr. Dale went to the crate and said calmly, "Certainly. We keep the tools with the box for convenience. Shall I?" He slid a small panel of the crate's wooden frame, which opened up a tray. Inside was a weird tool—a screwdriver on one end, a hammer on the other—and a few extra nails.

As he pried the lid loose, I caught a glimpse of Rob, Reece, and Dr. Eloise on the other side of the security gate, looking worried. I said to Dr. Dale, "I'll go tell the others."

The security guard stepped in my path. "Stay right here!"

"Oh, sorry. Sure."

Marcus shot me a "you idiot" look. The people going through the gate gaped at us like we were criminals caught in the act. My face burned. I wanted to tell Dr. Dale that there was a blade in the crate, but didn't want to arouse more suspicion. *Is there a secret compartment in the bottom? Did someone put a sword in the box to smuggle it through? How'd they do it with us right there? Or is it the sword of the Lord, invisible to the eye? Dr. Dale is so calm. . . . Does he know something?*

The lid came off. The guards lifted out the armor, spilling packing straw on the airport floor. They unwrapped and examined it piece by piece. Dr. Dale explained it was an antiquity and must be handled very carefully. He thanked them for wearing gloves. They emptied the crate to the last shred of straw. There was no sword. I kept my mouth shut.

"There was a weapon in here," said the security guard.

Dr. Dale looked confused. "Excuse me?"

"A sword blade showed on the scanner."

Dr. Dale looked into the crate, baffled. "Impossible."

My voice trembled, "I saw it. There was a blade."

Dr. Dale looked at the dismembered armor scattered on packing straw. His face slowly changed from confusion to suspicion to astonishment. He whispered to himself, "He speaks the Word, and he is the Word." Then, "He has the sword, and he *is* the sword." He turned to the guard with a strange smile on his face. "Scan it again, please, piece by piece."

They moved us to an unused security gate so the other passengers could go on through. They fired up the scanner, laid the helmet aside, and ran the other pieces through, one at a time. The breastplate showed bits of metal: the torq, the brads. They ran the belt with its disc-shaped pieces, then the shield, which showed a metal piece roughly the size of a hot dog. One of the shoes of peace went through. Nothing. The last shoe went through. The conveyor belt stopped.

"There!" my voice cracked. "There it is!"

The guard looked at the shoe, then the screen. He pulled the shoe out and examined it.

Dr. Dale said with pleasant enthusiasm, "Why, this is wonderful! I'm sorry for the disturbance, sir, but we have been looking for this piece and thought it lost. Yes! Quite often the ancient warrior would conceal a weapon. Eureka!" He said lightly to me, "We have found it." Then to the guard, "If you kindly allow me a penknife, I'll extract the item so we may all have a look. If you need to contact a higher authority, please do. Again, I apologize, and I thank you."

Dr. Eloise looked worriedly at her watch and came over toward us, keeping her distance. "Dear, the flight leaves in fifteen minutes, and we are at gate thirty-three." She asked the guard, "Can you please let the children go on? This is an international flight, their first trip to Japan."

"Please stay back, ma'am," the guard barked. Two more guards showed up with handguns and walkie-talkies and made us all take seats—Dr. Dale, Marcus, and me separate from the others. I was ready to explode. *We have the sword!*

Borrowing gloves and a Swiss army knife from the armed guard who kept his hand near his gun, Dr. Dale studied the foot-and-a-half-long shin guard. He ran his fingers along the inside. At the bottom was a leather hem folded under metal trim. He snipped a few threads and stepped back while the guard carefully drew out a slim sword blade.

"There you have it," Dr. Dale said conclusively, and went on as if taking mental notes, "It is plain, but elegantly so, about fourteen inches long. Can't pinpoint the age from the style." To the security guard in charge he said, "Mystery solved. Once again I apologize. If I'd known, I would have certainly applied for special clearance."

"It's a concealed weapon, sir," said the guard. "You were taking it into the cabin." He looked at the Stallards' passports and asked questions about Antiquities Research Center. I wanted to offer to stay behind. I wondered where the rest of the sword was, if it was hidden in the armor. I wanted to touch the blade and test the edge for sharpness. It had to be the sword of the Lord. It just had to!

Everything happened in a rush. A supervisor told the Stallards they'd have to fill out some papers and go on a later flight. They ran us all through security again. Dr. Eloise asked again if we "children" would be allowed to go on. We objected, but Dr. Eloise pleaded with the guard, "Please, sir, let them make their flight. They are students, not employed by our business." She looked at her watch again fretfully. "Oh, they have six minutes and a disabled girl!"

Dr. Dale turned to us matter-of-factly. "Mei will meet you in Osaka. We'll catch the next flight and come directly to Nikko. Here's the information you need." He pressed a note in my hand. "You have the necessary addresses and phone numbers. Remain calm. We'll see you in Nikko."

The guard let the four of us through and called ahead to hold the plane. He got Reece a shuttle cart; we guys threw our backpacks on and jogged along behind. They rushed us to the departure gate and hurried us onto the jet. As we were getting settled, I read Dr. Dale's scratched-out note, then passed it on for the others: *Excellent composure! Withhold judgment—and euphoria—until the evidence on our find is collected. Leave no related correspondence in the seat pockets.*

"Brilliant," Rob said, dropping into the seat beside me.

"Yeah!" I thought he meant the sword hidden in the armor of God. Way cool. The quest was complete!

Rob glared sourly at the seat in front of him.

"What?" I asked.

"I looked back one last time before we turned the corner to the concourse. The Stallards were shaking hands with the security guard and smiling."

"So?"

"I mean, like a mission-accomplished handshake." He looked at me and whispered, "Where's the diamond?"

"I have it."

"On you?"

"In my backpack. In the overhead compartment."

"Do they know that?"

I remembered how Dr. Eloise had patted the helmet when I told her the gem was safe. "Probably not."

He gave me a sly, sneaky look. "You outwitted them."

"No, I just . . . wait, you don't think it was a setup?!"

He roughly buckled himself in. "You saw how they pushed the idea of taking the armor at the last minute, so we couldn't say no. What if they'd already figured out where the sword was? Sometimes archaeologists x-ray artifacts in the lab. What if this was their way of getting the whole thing after all?"

I remembered how casual Dr. Eloise was that we hadn't found the sword, how odd that seemed. Maybe they were just trying to find a way to get the diamond. But . . . "No," I said solidly. "They didn't ditch us. They wouldn't. If they'd wanted it, they'd have taken the whole thing before."

Rob growled, "We knew where they lived before, but they've cleared out their Chicago office. They say they live in Boston, but all we have is a P.O. box. By the time we get to Osaka, they could be in Istanbul with our armor!" He snorted. "At least you have the diamond."

Seconds before the plane started taxiing, a young couple came rushing back and filled the two empty seats behind us, the seats which I'd thought were for the Stallards.

Preoccupied with getting her stuff in order, Reece leaned across Marcus and said, "Hey, remember what Dr. Eloise said taking off to Ireland: 'We're in God's hands now!'"

They're not ditching us in Japan. After all this? They're not!

Nobody mentioned the sword, because Dr. Dale had said to withhold judgment. Marcus and Reece hadn't heard

Rob's comments about the diamond, but every so often he and I exchanged knowing glances. I could tell he was holding back all kinds of bad feelings, especially the kind of anger that goes along with being played for a sucker.

We changed planes in Chicago and then settled in for a long flight with headphones, our inflatable flight pillows, and skimpy blankets. There was a meal and a movie. Over Alaska Reece switched seats and gave Marcus the end so he could sleep while she and I played cards.

"Hey," I said as she shuffled the deck, "that dream about the threatening flower. That mean anything to you?"

"No. You?"

"No."

"It's probably nothing," she said. "Japan's safer than the States. Everybody has weird dreams sometimes."

"Yeah."

"Changing the subject," she said, "a few more hours and we'll be there! I can't wait! Mei has a whole bunch of fun things for us to do. There's a resort town she wants to take us to, and we can swim in a stream near her house. Their church is having a picnic for us!"

Forgetting our troubles for a minute, I grabbed her ponytail, pulled her face toward mine, and rubbed noses with her. An Eskimo kiss.

She giggled. "What are you doing!?"

"We're over Alaska."

Eleven hours in the air. I couldn't sleep; my legs were cramped. Rob's suspicions rubbed off on me. *With so much at stake—all the time—will we ever trust the Stallards? Ever? Will I see the sword again? Get to hold it? What if, after all this time and danger and hard work and waiting . . ."*

The only good thing about the long flight was Reece asleep on my shoulder.

The captain's voice came over the loudspeaker: "Afternoon, folks. We'll be coming in behind a typhoon as it veers north across the main island. Not a big one, but it's leaving an arm of fairly high winds. We can expect significant turbulence. Nothing to worry about; we're in touch with the tower and will get you to Osaka safely. You'll want to finish your drinks and buckle in."

No kidding. The flight attendants took their seats, and for the next half hour we got bounced around like a toddler on his grandpa's knee; only it was no fun at all, and nobody was singing "Pony Boy." Marcus forgot everything he'd learned at the Cliffs of Morte about height fright.

Rob grabbed the airsick bag from the seat pocket and read the names for *puking* in eight languages. A nice delicate shade of green, he said, "If they don't get us through this storm soon, look out for *luftkrankheit!*"

We dipped below the storm clouds, and a square of concrete the size of a postage stamp appeared in the bay of a huge gray city. The plane rocked and shuddered and dipped. I prayed that we'd make the runway in one piece.

Chapter 5

IT was strange being in a country where everything was spoken in another language and where most everybody was shorter and darker than me. I began to see what Mei had felt, being a foreigner in a strange land. We followed the crowd off the plane into the terminal. We made it okay through customs by doing what everyone else did. Mei was waiting for us behind a wall of windows.

Marcus took one look at her and wheezed, "Whoa!"

She was taller, her hair longer and streaked with red. She had on skinny jeans, high heels, and a flowery top. Mei was a knockout. She waved wildly when she spotted us. Once through the door, Reece dropped her bag and crutch. They did the usual squealy-huggy girl stuff, and then Mei hugged us guys. We couldn't believe we were all together again.

Mei peered through the window back into the terminal. "Where are the Stallards?"

I shot Rob a "keep quiet" glance. "They're coming later."

Mei helped us exchange our money for yen. Then she said to Marcus, "We are taking *shinkansen,* just like you wished in Council Cave! Our dream comes true!"

We hauled our stuff into the bottom storage bin of a big tall bus and boarded. It was so crowded there were no two seats together. For an hour we plowed through jammed traffic across the biggest city I'd ever been in, downtown in all directions as far as the eye could see. At the next terminal, I carried Reece's backpack while Mei led us through a swarm of people, like Christmas rush—times a hundred. At the bullet train office, we stood in line for a half hour and filled out papers for rail passes. Then we walked more, went through turnstiles, and climbed a crowded flight of steps to the train platform. Mei bought us way cool little drinks from vending machines and gave us gifts.

Watching down the tracks, Marcus grinned, "See what I mean, my people? Here she comes: classiest land transit in the world." An enormous, gleaming white, ultra modern projectile coasted in and stopped. The door of the *shinkansen* slid open. We hauled ourselves and our luggage onto the train, stashed our stuff in the overheads, and turned the plush blue seats around to face each other. I sat the other four together and I put myself right across the aisle. Reece was all smiles. Rob looked a little dazed. Marcus couldn't take his eyes off Mei.

"This trip is four hundred miles," Mei told us.

"I'm sleeping!" said Rob.

Not crazy about sitting for several more hours after a whole day on a plane, I went exploring. The bullet train had a dozen cars with restrooms and changing rooms, vending machines with all kinds of drinks, and even phone booths with desks where you could do office work—all super clean, super modern. I'd pictured countries in The Window as being primitive, people living in shacks and doing laundry in a river (not that I thought Mei lived that way). But this beat anything I'd seen in the States.

A voice over the PA said we were departing for Tokyo.

Mei clapped her hands together. "I have three weeks with my friends! No school and only two papers to write."

"Homework?" Reece cried. "You have to do homework?!"

"It is okay. Not too much. Tell me what is happening in my American town and who has driver's license?"

"I do," Marcus said smirking. "We'll do a road trip when you come back: Yosemite, the Rockies, the Canyon . . ."

Show-off.

By the time we'd told Mei about the blade discovered in the scanner at the airport—all of us sure it was the sword of the Lord—we were clipping along at one hundred seventy miles an hour. It didn't feel fast, just a supersilky ride, but fields and phone poles went by in a blur. When we passed another bullet train on a parallel track, it felt like our train had been swatted with a giant pillow. *Pfoom!* Rob was fascinated by the Doppler effect created by two trains passing at a combined speed of three hundred forty miles per hour.

"Don't stick your head out the window to study it, Rob," Reece joked sarcastically.

"I'm not an idiot."

Marcus smiled coolly at Mei. "No, he's a ninja."

She gasped at Rob. "You are studying martial arts?"

"Acting," Reece explained, and proceeded to tell about Rob's stunt in Gilead.

We cracked up all over again. Rob acted put out with us, but he was fine being the center of attention.

Smiling at Rob thoughtfully, Mei said, "We must give you a ninja name then: Shinobu." She wrote down the *kanji*. "This means a person doing something secret, hidden."

Marcus snorted, "Oh, right. Secret man."

We all wanted Japanese names, and Mei said she'd think up some.

Zipping up the coast of Japan, we took turns telling Mei about life in Magdeline. Reece had written about my baptism, but I told her about Rob's rubber ducky trick.

A lady in a white uniform appeared at the end door of our car with a snack cart, said something in Japanese, and bowed. Mei bought us pricey snacks: green tea ice cream and sea chicken *onigiri*: rice balls with tuna inside.

Rob was all intrigued by the drink boxes. "These straws telescope out to twice their length and have a joint so they bend!" He put on a straw demonstration then grudgingly said, "Japan's straw technology is more advanced than ours. So is their train technology."

Mei and Rob took pictures. The landscape changed from mountains and seascapes to another enormous city, crammed together while spreading out in all directions: Tokyo. We switched out to another bullet train, hurrying through another crush of people in huge underground tunnels lined with shops and restaurants.

"Rush hour!" Mei yelled as we pressed through the turnstile.

I didn't think it could be more crowded than Osaka, but it was. For a guy like me used to being alone a lot, this was way too much city.

Shooting north across the Kanto Plain, we headed into a range of dark, misty mountains drilled through with tunnels that were miles long, and Mei gave us our Japanese names. "Reece, you will be Mayu. It means true and kind." She turned to Marcus shyly. "You are cool, so I call you Ryo. And, Elijah," she smiled at me, "you are Takumi. It means pioneer and sea, since you have led your clan to explore across two oceans."

As the bullet rain slowed, Shinobu Wingate showed us on the map how far we'd gone in practically no time.

Mei said, "We switch trains now to a slow train. We will get to Nikko at night."

The local train was like a subway, with seats along the sides and empty space in the middle for people to stand. The rhythmic *clickety-clack* and the drain of jet lag (plus thirty hours with little sleep) suddenly got to me. I tried to stay awake planning what to do in case Rob was right about the Stallards. I personally couldn't believe they'd orchestrate a scam at the airport to give themselves a head start and make off with our armor into the wild blue yonder. True, they probably figured I'd stashed the diamond in the helmet for safekeeping. They thought they had it. But they didn't.

Rob nudged me awake as we pulled into Nikko; I'd fallen asleep on my backpack. Our train had emptied out along the way; we were the last ones in our car. The station was old and small, the opposite of the bustling stations of Osaka and Tokyo.

Mei got directions to the inn from the guy in the ticket window. "He said it is a short walk."

We stepped out into the dark, five high school kids in a strange village nestled in wooded mountains. Mei warned Reece, "The sidewalk has holes and a drainage ditch underneath. If your crutch goes in a hole, you will fall."

Rob was talking to Marcus in a low voice, and I knew why: he was spilling his suspicions, even though I'd told him not to. Their muttering stopped after a while when we had to use all our energy for hauling ourselves up the narrow sidewalk. Thirty minutes later we were still trudging. Mei stopped at an intersection and looked around uneasily.

"Are we lost?" Rob asked.

"I don't think so," she answered. "A little farther."

I could hardly see Reece's face in the dark and thought about stopping for a snack to give her a rest. But the town seemed closed down for the night.

Marcus came up and said under his breath, "Global conference, huh?"

"Hey, your dad okayed this!" I griped back. The lonely street was a far cry from Dr. Eloise's fancy pamphlet with the picture of a cruise ship on the front and aerial shots of mountains and seashore advertising the conference.

Rob asked worriedly, "Elijah, are we even in the right town?"

"It is there!" Mei said cheerfully. "The *ryokan!* The inn!"

I'd been imagining a convention center like in downtown Columbus. But across the street, wedged between little darkened shop fronts, stood a big, gloomy, unpainted house backed up to a steep mountainside. The parking lot had room for three small cars.

"That's it?!" Rob whined what I was thinking.

I nudged him and shook my head. I didn't want Mei to feel like we were slamming her country. But I was already thinking, *Okay, if the Stallards don't show, we hole up in the same room for safety's sake, then head back at first light for Osaka. Thank God we have Mei to help us get home.* I don't mind saying I felt more lost than being stranded in Telanoo in a soupy fog.

We hauled our gear across the street to the inn. *So what if I never see the armor of God again? The whole point has been about its message, right? Salvation and faith and peace? Truth and righteousness? But . . . what if I lose that? What if the Stallards' story about the armor of God was all a big lie to get the diamond? Or what if this was a global kidnapping scheme and we never see home again?* Crazy, shadowy doubts swept through my mind.

Mei got us signed in while we dropped down and kicked off our shoes in the entry. The innkeeper, a friendly old woman with yellow teeth, talked Japanese a mile a minute as she led us up dimly lit back stairs. The guys' room was musty and low ceilinged, with tatami mat floors. Thin mattresses were stacked in the corner beside a low table holding the oldest TV I'd ever seen. We dumped our gear while the lady took the girls down the hall.

Inspecting the room, Rob suddenly burst out laughing. "Look at this sign: 'Prease keep door close. There is a bug.'" He eased open the paper doors, then the glass sliding doors beyond them. "Hey, there's a little garden out here. Wait . . . how can that be? We're on the second floor."

Foggy-brained and dog-tired, I peered out into the darkness and wondered if we were in another dimension.

Marcus said knowingly, "Guys, the inn's built into the mountainside."

"Oh yeah," Rob and I said in unison.

Rob tried the TV, and Marcus plopped down on the pile of mattresses. I put on the outdoor slippers, stepped out into the dark garden, and closed the doors behind me—to keep the bug out. Sounds of the guys talking inside faded. To my left was a little *torii* about three feet high. A few feet beyond it and surrounded by baby trees was a tiny building. It was a creepy sort of cute. I felt like a giant. *A gate to the gods. I'll tell Reece. Wonder what's in the little house?* I knelt down, ducked my head under the gate, and looked down the little path into the doorway of the building. Staring back at me was a living, blinking human eye.

Chapter 6

※※

I fell back and gasped. A couple of seconds of hard breathing and staring at the building—which was big enough to hold a human head—gave me the guts to look again. The eye blinked! Just as I blinked. *It's a mirror! A reflection of my own eye!* Feeling skittish and dumb, I chuckled to myself and went back inside where the guys were making their pallets for the night. Then we went down the hall to the girls' room.

Mei obviously figured I didn't know what to do next and took over. "Now you are in my country, and I will be the host, okay? It is custom to take *ofuro* at night. The boys' bath is down the hall, the girls' bath is on the third floor. Then you wear *yukata*." She picked up a stack of folded, blue-patterned robes. "Use as a robe or pajamas—you can even wear it outside. We will have tea. And you can go to sleep while I wait for the Stallards to come."

Revived by a hot bath and feeling sort of spiffy in my Japanese getup, I walked down the hallway listening to see if the Stallards had come. Quiet. Even down in the lobby and up the old wooden stairs to the third floor, there was no TV blaring, no talking. *Where are all the other convention people? Are we the only ones at the inn?* I'd planned on spending some time alone with Reece that night but had second thoughts about splitting up the group. I figured Reece and Mei would be scared, but they were busy giggling at us guys in our robes. I warned Shinobu not to turn ninja and vandalize the paper screens. He did a few moves anyway and accidentally hit a low-hanging ceiling light, which went swinging wildly.

Marcus shook his head and said, "We can't take you anywhere," and sidled up to Mei.

Honestly, I was fried. And peeved at the guys. But sitting around a low table on a straw mat floor with matching robes and a pot of tea, we really looked like a clan. A strong hope welled up in me. *With or without the Stallards*, I thought fiercely, *with or without the armor, even tired and lost and sitting in a musty room, dead tired after thirty hours of travel, six thousand miles from home, still . . . I'm living a dream.*

Morning comes early in Japan. Sunlight filtered through the paper door around 5:00. I lay there for a good half hour unable to sleep because, to my body, it was 4:00 in the afternoon. I got dressed, crept down the hall, listened at the girls' door, and heard two people breathing evenly. *Sound asleep. Safe.* I went downstairs to the entryway. The door was slid wide open to the street, cars and bicycles whizzing past. In the night, someone had lined up our shoes all facing out. I was surprised no one had stolen them. There were other shoes too, other guests. *So we're not alone,* I thought optimistically. Then I noticed next to my sneakers a familiar pair of sandals. *Dr. Dale! They're here! They're here, and the armor's here! They didn't ditch us!*

I stepped out into the sunshine and breathed in the smell of car exhaust mixed with fresh mountain air and frying fish. My shadows and doubts faded. I headed left down the village street to work the kinks out of my body from yesterday's travels. *Thanks, God, for the day and for getting us here. And for where you're going to lead us, thank you!*

Several blocks later the shops thinned out. Ahead in the morning mist was a bridge above a stream full of big boulders. I crossed the bridge, climbed down the bank, sat on a rock in the middle, and got out my Quella. Pearly light filtered through the trees. Clear water rushed past me, all around me. *Yep. Living a dream.* With no special devo in mind, I looked up the word *stream* and scrolled down to Psalms, the *Warrior:* "As the deer pants for streams of water, so my soul pants for you, O God. My soul thirsts for God, for the living God. When can I go and meet with God?"

Thirsting for God? I thought back to Gilead, the days without water, and tried to compare it with wanting to know God. *Just being honest here, El-Telan-Yah. Sure, I want to know you better . . . but I can't say it gnaws at me like the thirst I had in Gilead. Is that wrong?*

Back at the inn, I was taking off my shoes when here came a pair of old bare feet down the steep steps at the end of the hallway. Dr. Eloise's whole self descended in a

THE CARPET OF BONES

wine-colored dress and ran to me like she hadn't seen me in decades. "We are here! We arrived before midnight."

"How'd you get here so fast?" I asked.

"Direct flight," she said simply. "The others are awake."

Familiar voices came from the top of the steps. Pairs of feet, then legs, then whole selves came down, wondering where in blazes I'd been. Reece cried, "We were worried!"

"I was down by the river talking to God. The coffee shop is two doors down. Let's go."

Our first meal in Japan was a traditional breakfast of miso soup, rice, a little fish (whole, with the head and eyes), a pile of cabbage, and green tea.

Rob made an eensy hat from his napkin and put it over the fish's head because, as he said, "I can't eat something that's staring at me!"

Looking offended, Marcus said, "Try to blend in, Shinobu. Don't embarrass Mei."

"I'm not!" he snipped. "I'm just joking."

Six days in Gilead had taught me a lot of things, one being to be grateful for anything edible. It was pretty good. Actually, I could have eaten two breakfasts, the way my body was whining, *Dinnertime was hours ago, Creek!*

While the clan jabbered away about the rough landing and the bullet train, I worried over the Tear of Blood. I got ready to bring it up, but Dr. Eloise said, "Children, we mentioned in a letter about our friend's dream." She took a minute to retell the flower dream to Mei. "Our friend continues to be unsettled regarding our trip. She is quite the spiritual warrior, so we do trust her. If you have stumbled across anything in your preparations, we'd appreciate hearing it."

We looked blank. I said no for all of us.

Back at the *ryokan,* which looked more shabby than scary in the light of day, Dr. Eloise said with a wink, "I see we have stumbled upon another no-shamrock inn. But we shall make the best of it. Now we must prepare for the day. We'll examine our favorite relic and storm a stronghold!"

While we waited for the girls to fix their hair and stuff, I showed Dr. Dale the little building out my door. "Why's there a mirror in that little temple?" I asked.

He glanced at it and murmured something in a foreign language. "It's called a shrine, Elijah. The presence of a mirror comes from the legend of the sun goddess, the premier deity in Japan. She and her brother, the storm god, weren't getting along, so she hid in a cave, plunging the world into darkness. The other gods used a mirror and a pearl necklace to lure her out. She saw herself in the mirror, was overcome by her own splendor, and emerged."

"But when you look in that shrine, you see yourself. It's like you're the god."

Dr. Stallard said grimly, "Yes. And that's how it is all over the world."

The Stallards had already unpacked the armor pieces and laid them out on a sleeping mat. I knelt down and carefully picked up the blade in my two hands. I felt the cold metal, ran my thumb across the sharp edge. "Clean, efficient, the perfect size."

"Amazingly sharp," said Dr. Dale. "If the blade was in one piece of the armor, we may speculate that the other parts are hidden as well. Why don't each of you take a piece and examine it."

Rob said authoritatively, "We'll be looking for a scabbard, a hand guard, and a hilt."

Casually I picked up the helmet. I needed to see if the diamond's former hiding place had been dug out again. Because if it had, it would prove to me that the Stallards had followed us to Japan to get what they were really after: the Tear of Blood. In a way, I didn't want to know. But I had to know. I looked inside. The cavity behind the center of the forehead was smooth, intact. Nobody had messed with it. I sighed in relief and glanced at the Stallards. They were smiling over us kids like we were their grandkids and it was Christmas.

Mei picked up the belt, holding it carefully in the same way as when she first found it on Devil's Cranium.

Rob reached over and felt the disc-shaped ornaments of the belt. "Hand guard!" he said. "The metal pieces are hand guards!"

Reece cried, *"Sugoi*, Mei! *Sugoi!"*

Marcus said deeply, "The whole sword has been with us the entire time. . . ."

Mei loosened the metal pieces from their leather laces and nested one in the other to make a solid piece with a hole in the middle where the blade fit through. "It is the hand guard!"

Marcus took the breastplate and felt along the back. "Hand me the blade, will you?" He slipped the sword tip along the side seam, cutting a few stitches to get a couple of fingers in. "There are leather reinforcements fastened in the back, but one piece moves." He cut a few more stitches, slipped his hand in, and drew out a piece of thick leather. It was shaped almost like a pair of pants with pointy legs. He folded it, lining up the points and old stitching holes. Losing his usual cool, he said, "Look, people, see the slits where it can be connected to the belt of truth! We have a scabbard!"

Dr. Eloise got out a travel-size sewing kit to stitch the scabbard together.

I couldn't find any removable piece on the helmet.

Reece cut a few stitches along the bottom of the shin guard and worked out a long strip of folded leather.

Rob said, "That's for winding around the grip. Who has the grip?"

A little more searching and Marcus found the hot-dog-shaped hand grip inside the shield, masquerading as armband reinforcement. For the next hour Rob and Dr. Dale put the sword together piece by piece. They knew a lot about how to assemble it. (I was always a bow and arrow guy myself.) Every part had been hidden in the armor.

When it was together, Dr. Dale laid it across my open hands, me being the head of the clan. "The sword of the Lord, Elijah."

For a long moment I just stared at it. Sure, the sword wasn't a whole lot to look at. It wasn't huge, didn't have much in the way of ornamentation. Just a no-nonsense blade to be used at short range. "It's easy to handle, lightweight."

Reece reached for the hilt. "Even I could use it." She held it up in front of her and smiled at me so deep it felt like a slug in the chest. "We did it, Elijah, we did it! We have the full armor of God!"

"Who can know," Dr. Eloise whispered eerily, "what fires have forged its steel?" While the others passed the sword around, I excused myself, went to my room, and closed the door. I'd never cried from joy before. Never. But I cried like a baby.

When I'd collected myself, I went back. Reece was quoting a verse, "'In the beginning was the Word, and the Word was with God, and the Word was God.' He speaks the Word, and he *is* the Word. It's so mysterious . . ."

Marcus thought out loud, "Every piece of God's sword is made from every piece of his armor. And vice versa."

Rob said, "Except for the helmet. You didn't find anything, did you, Elijah?"

"No. But the sword is complete."

"Where's the word on it?" Reece asked.

We looked but couldn't find it. Reece scowled.

Rob said, "The hand guard is a little loose."

Mei studied it. "Maybe I don't have it put together right. It needs tighter."

"But it is the sword of the Lord," I announced. "It has to be, even without a word inscribed on it."

Reece looked doubtful. "The other pieces were inscribed."

Rob suggested, "Maybe it's microscopic. Those words engraved on the mesh were small—"

Dr. Eloise broke in, "We never would have found them without the linen tester," and went fishing in her luggage again. Unfolding the little square magnifying glass, she gave the sword a quick once-over. "I see nothing in the way of letters or symbols."

We took turns reexamining the sword.

Mei said, "With samurai warriors, the secret wisdom of the clan might be carved in the blade in very small letters or hidden inside, even inside the metal on a piece of paper."

"Inside the blade?" I asked. "How would you get it out?"

"You must break the blade."

"We're not doing that!" I barked. "No."

For a long minute we sat on the mat floor with armor pieces scattered around, the sword gleaming in the morning sun.

Rob asked hesitantly, not wanting to seem dumb, "So . . . what's it mean, now that we have the whole armor of God?"

Putting away the linen tester and sewing kit, Dr. Eloise said, "Actually there is one more piece."

Our mouths dropped open. Our eyes got wide.

Rob whined, "Another piece?! You gotta be kidding me!!"

We were on the brink of freaking out. Reece grabbed her Bible and flipped it open to Ephesians chapter 6. "Okay, it says belt of truth, breastplate of righteousness, shoes of peace, shield of faith, helmet of salvation . . . 'and the sword of the Spirit, which is the word of God.'"

"Read on," said Dr. Eloise.

"'And pray in the Spirit on all occasions with all kinds of prayers and requests.'"

"Prayer's a *piece?*" Rob asked.

"Thank goodness!" I dropped back onto the pillows. No more vague clues, no more digging in hard clay or scuba diving in Silver Lake, no more reaching into burning cars, or run-ins with creepy guys like Dowland or Theobald.

Dr. Dale said to me in a fatherly tone, "Not so fast there, Elijah. You've given your life to the almighty one, all of you children have. You left the enemy camp for the eternal kingdom. You have blessing and power in this life and glory in the life to come. But now you have become the enemy's enemy. There are hazards."

Dr. Eloise jumped in. "To take your communiqués from the Almighty too lightly is to be unprepared for the trials. Prayer is like this stitching that holds the armor together. Drop a stitch here and there and finally the thing unravels."

"So the armor won't work without prayer," Reece said.

"Correct," answered Dr. Dale. "To use another metaphor:

what good is a lamp if you don't plug it in?"

Dr. Eloise pressed her hands together. "Not to intrude on your spiritual journeys, children, but we would like to hear about the preparations you made and what you have learned."

Reece said, "I've been fasting one day a week. I read through Psalms several times. I prayed."

"And what did you pray about, dear?"

"That I'd be able to come, that I'd be ready for whatever happened. I prayed for Mei a lot. For her church."

"Very good." Dr. Eloise looked around at all of us. "You know what to expect when you engage in spiritual warfare?" She waited for an answer.

Marcus said, "We take 'em down!"

Dr. Dale smiled patiently. "Yes. That's exactly what we do. But it is an invisible war. Our ultimate goal is rescuing people, not wielding power. Faith, not force."

Marcus said, "Got it. Our battle isn't against flesh and blood, but against the powers of the dark world and evil forces in the heavenly realms."

Mei sat listening.

Rob said sheepishly, "I gave up snacks and drinks like pop. Is that fasting?" He added for extra bonus points, "And I go to church and Bible studies. And I know Japanese history!"

Dr. Dale said, "There are no hard-and-fast rules for preparation except that it must be done in the right spirit.

Fasting and prayer are about discipline, thinking more about God than you do yourself."

Dr. Eloise turned to Mei. "Dear, we know you are very new to all this. We don't expect for you—"

Mei broke in, "Yes, but Reece talked to me in letters. I read the Bible and prayed at my church or in my room. I did not change my eating because my aunt will worry about me. And many girls in Japan starve themselves to be thin, so I couldn't stop eating at school; it would be a bad example."

Dr. Eloise looked at her sympathetically. "Your walk with God is a lonely one, isn't it, child?"

Trying to hide her sadness, Mei said, "A little bit."

"Courageous girl," said Dr. Eloise. "Most excellent girl!"

The Stallards wanted to hear about my preparations next. I gave them a pat answer: prayer and Bible study and stuff. Hey, after Gilead I figured I was ready for anything.

Dr. Dale instructed, "Today you will all observe. Take your Bibles—your swords. Don't engage if you don't want to. It's a fascinating cultural site with spectacular architecture; you can simply be tourists."

"A few from the conference will join us!" chirped Dr. Eloise. "You will meet the SOS, and we predict you will get along splendidly." She stood—a signal that we were on our way. "Expect the unexpected, children. We must put on the full armor of God in our hearts and minds. For today we go through the gates. Today we begin."

Chapter 7

WE headed out from the old mountainside inn and made a left through town. We stopped for vending machine drinks, and Dr. Eloise warned Reece about the holes in the narrow sidewalk. She cautioned all of us about the traffic as if we were grade-schoolers: "When crossing a street, remember to look right first, then left, then right again. Traffic comes from the right because they drive on the left."

"To the left, to the left!" Dr. Dale made fun of himself, strolling along with his skinny can of coffee milk. "As much international driving as I have done over the years, I still get confused. In the Orient one drives on the left. In America it's the right. Most of Europe is right, but Britain is left. Turkey is right. Pakistan is left."

We went down the street singing to help Dr. Dale remember which side to drive on: "To the left, to the left, to the left left left. . . ."

Nikko was an old, quaint mountain village. Dr. Eloise said, "It has a bit of morose, nostalgic appeal, I suppose. The valley setting is superb, isn't it, Dale? Couldn't we live happily here? Fresh air, fresh food, mountain strolls. Good for the constitution. Mei, the Japanese are the longest-lived people in the world, are they not?"

Dr. Dale asked what we knew of the history of the place.

Rob piped up, "It's a shrine to a dynasty that unified Japan under one government four hundred years ago."

"Exactly, and that was a good thing," commented Dr. Dale. "But in the process, they tortured and executed untold thousands of people, particularly believers."

"Not a good thing!" Rob huffed.

"Certainly not. At this shrine those very leaders are worshiped as supernatural representatives of the sun goddess. To worship a created thing—whether man or beast or element of nature—is breaking God's first Commandment: 'I am the LORD your God. . . . You shall have no other gods before me.'"

Dr. Eloise broke in. "An offense to the creator! But he does not forbid such a thing because he needs our adoration."

Reece said, "He just knows how the universe works."

"Precisely. When you worship something, you give it your power—the power and love meant to grow between you and the Father, to give purpose to life. Worshiping other gods is the absolute worst thing you can do!"

Rob asked, "I'm not disagreeing, but . . . why the worst?"

"Because making something your god opens the door!"

"The door?" I asked.

"The veil! The veil to the evil one and his vast hordes! No human should give his power to a created thing! The spiritual world is not a safe place, no matter what naive seer, diviner, or medium says to the contrary. Those on the dark side are shape-shifters, mask-wearers! Do not be fooled."

We crossed the bridge where I'd had devos that morning and stopped at an intersection at the foot of a broad mountain. From the right came a group of foreigners.

Dr. Eloise waved and said, "There are our early birds!"

We joined up at a wide spot in the path overlooking the stream. We milled around and introduced ourselves. There were a handful of adult conference people and more than a dozen teens, the SOS. I caught a few names: Robin was a tall, pretty girl with brown hair. Karinna had green eyes, wild red hair, a long skirt, and bare feet. They were from the States. Eva from Germany was short and athletic. The guys were Li, a Taiwanese with perfect English; Dmitri from Ukraine; a scrawny kid from Hawaii named Cody; and Mahesh from India. The leader of the SOS was a blond woman in her forties wearing a navy T-shirt that said "Pilgrimage" on the back. Her name was Veronica.

Dr. Dale—by far the oldest guy—led the way. We followed a path above the stream for a few blocks, and then he turned and stopped us. "This is where we engage . . . and turn the battle over to the Lord."

Suddenly I got nervous. I had no idea what was about to happen. For the sake of my clan, I acted relaxed, slugging down the last of my skinny can of peach nectar.

He read from 2 Chronicles 20, where a king facing an unbeatable army made singers form the front lines to praise God. Before the battle even began, the enemy troops got confused and turned their swords on each other. When the good army got to the battlefield, all they saw were corpses.

Dr. Dale read, "'This is what the LORD says to you: "Do not be afraid or discouraged because of this vast army. For the battle is not yours, but God's."'" Then he lifted his eyes to the skies and powerfully barked, "'The word of God is living and active. Sharper than any double-edged sword, it penetrates even to dividing soul and spirit.' Your Word is truth!"

Walking up a winding road, the conference people sang the names of God and the power of Jesus. I'd heard some of the music at my church and in Ireland. We had no weapons, but it sort of seemed we really were going into battle.

Veronica reminded the SOS kids and us too, "This is a tourist site, and we are guests in another country. We respect their beliefs even if we do not agree with them."

Marcus whispered to me, "She sounds like my mom."

"And don't draw attention to yourself. If fear overtakes you, pair up, stop, and pray. Use the weapons he gives you."

I glanced questioningly at Reece.

"We're observing," she said uncertainly.

Then we were on a long, wide gravel avenue lined with huge evergreens. Ahead stood a *torii* like the one outside my room. Only this one was stone, thirty feet high, and massive.

"'This is the gate of the LORD, through which the righteous may enter,'" Reece said shakily.

Li, the sharp-looking Taiwanese, came up beside her: "'Lift up your heads, O you gates; be lifted up, you ancient doors, that the King of glory may come in. Who is this

King of glory? The LORD strong and mighty, the LORD mighty in battle. . . . He is the King of glory.'"

He smiled. "That's my job here—to pray that verse."

Shocked, Reece said, "I . . . I think it's . . . mine too."

Dr. Dale overheard and glanced back. "Reece, Li, you have your weapons."

Anyone who wanted could stay at the gate, so Reece paired off with Li and Veronica. Hesitantly I went on.

It didn't take long to get what was happening. A couple of the SOS kids zoned in at the purifying basin where people were washing their hands and mouths. They quietly flipped through their Bibles. "Here," one said to the other. "Isaiah 41:17."

I found it in the Quella and read to myself: "The poor and needy search for water, but there is none; their tongues are parched with thirst. But I the LORD will answer them; I, the God of Israel, will not forsake them." With open Bibles they prayed for the people trying to get pure enough to go into the shrine and worship a man.

Mingling among the tourists, admiring the cool buildings and ancient forest around us, we passed through another gateway to the gods, then another.

Ever the history buff, Rob whispered, "Can you believe it? These buildings have been here longer than America has been a country!"

Small groups casually split off and drifted in different directions. Inside one small building sat three beautiful gold and black containers about three or four feet square. Tourists were bowing and praying to the boxes. Mei was there, but she wasn't bowing. She felt me come up beside her and said, "The presence of the three gods is there."

"In those boxes?" I asked.

She nodded. We were quiet for a long time.

Finally she struggled to say, "It is very hard not to believe what my ancestors believed for many generations."

"I know. My parents don't believe the same as me either. And my ancestors were the MacMerrits!"

I strolled on to the last gate, which was unlike the others, a massive gatehouse with a roof. It was carved all around with hundreds of creatures, horned and fanged with bulging eyes; writhing dragons and demon dogs painted green and white with gaping, bloodred mouths. I didn't understand it. I couldn't take my eyes from it. I felt frozen in my tracks— rooted in the spot the same way I'd been two summers ago when I couldn't find Mei and was worried she'd gone over Lover's Leap. *Am I supposed to do something here?*

I looked around for someone else from the group. Several yards away and sitting on a step, Robin was reading her Bible. She looked up and spotted me. I motioned her over.

"Look at this," I said. "What's it mean? Why are there monsters in a temple?"

"Wow . . . ," Robin said, gazing up at the threshold to the inner shrine. "Wow."

"Yeah," I said grimly.

"I don't mean *them,*" she nodded to the demon dogs and dragons. "Guess what I just found, what I was just reading?"

"What?"

"'To the arrogant I say, "Boast no more," and to the wicked, "Do not lift up your horns. Do not lift your horns against heaven; do not speak with outstretched neck." No one from the east or the west or from the desert can exalt a man. But it is God who judges.'"

I got it. Now it was my turn. This was my battle post, and that verse was my weapon. I thought about the words. Then I said them . . . and said them again—still quiet but with more authority. I felt out of place and surrounded by an eerie quiet. Nothing happened—no earthquake or lightning from Heaven. Robin wandered off, but I stayed and prayed for a long while that no one would make a god of himself or for himself. I wandered among the shrine buildings, past clumps of people reading or talking to each other seriously. A few strolled around with deep, thoughtful expressions on their faces. They were activating the armor in their hearts, using the sword against an unseen enemy. Dr. Dale kept looking up toward the trees, as if listening.

We met back out under the first massive stone *torii,* everyone still drifting around, talking quietly. Dr. Dale asked, "Are we . . . finished?"

Most everyone nodded.

Karinna frowned at her bare feet. "Not yet. I keep

remembering a phrase—*build up, build up*—but that's all I know. It seems important."

"Coming up." Marcus flipped open his Quella and scrolled through a couple of verses. "This must be it. 'Pass through, pass through the gates! Prepare the way for the people. Build up, build up the highway! Remove the stones.'" He looked up at the giant gate towering over our heads, then at me with a wild twinkle in his eye. "Orders straight from headquarters, Takumi. How cool is that!"

Dr. Dale smiled. "I believe we are finished here. We pass through the gates."

We walked back down the ancient tree-lined avenue. I felt like I was floating on air. *That was it? That was spiritual warfare? It was so easy! No blood and guts, no screaming, at least not that I could hear. Just a peaceful spot in the mountains with big gates and cool old buildings.* We stopped at a snack shack. Dr. Dale bought himself an ice cream and a water bottle and sat down on a bench.

"So," I asked half joking, "did we win?"

"We've already won, Elijah. Good is eternal, evil is temporary, and that score was settled two thousand years ago. But the great deceiver, while he is permitted, still lusts for victims. His appetite is insatiable. Demonic insurgents under his control feed on pain and destruction. So, yes, the war is won, but the battles are not over. We press on with search-and-rescue missions, clearing the ancient rubble of fear and superstition. I believe that's what the verse meant about passing through the gate, building the highway, removing the stones." He glanced at the white sky above us.

"How do we know we accomplished anything?" I asked.

"First, we know by faith. You were wearing the shield of faith, weren't you?"

"Uh, yeah."

He finished up the ice cream. "Did you have any forebodings?"

"No."

"Some people do. Some don't." He sort of glowed with quiet confidence, smiled at the sky again, and said lightly, "I didn't think you would. Not today."

"Why?"

He wiped ice cream off his chin and leaned over to me. "See that open spot in the sky, beyond the gate?"

"Surrounded by the big trees? Yeah."

"The whole time, we had . . . protection. There."

"What do you mean?"

"An angel I suppose," he said wistfully. "In a circle above us."

"You saw it?!"

His eyes reflected white light from the sky. "With spiritual eyes, you might say."

He took a slug of his water bottle and said matter-of-factly, "If we succeeded, then we have aroused the enemy's anger. I can say with a fair amount of certainty that we will be attacked." He stood tiredly, gripping my shoulder to help himself up, and then looked down at me firmly. "Regardless, Elijah, you must pass through the gates and prepare the way. Remove the stones blocking the way of the people."

Down at the main road, most of the crowd was talking lunch, but the mountain stream was calling me. I got Dr. Dale's permission and headed down the bank, yelling at the others, "Come on! Let's cool off first!"

Soon, even the Stallards were picking their way down the bank and yanking their shoes off. The sun blazed, and there was no breeze in the valley, so my clan and the SOS cooled off by horsing around in the stream. We climbed on the warm rocks. Rob kept trying to sneak up on Marcus and get him in a hammerlock, but he had zero luck.

In a short while, one of the men came down the bank with a bag full of *bentous,* Japanese meals-in-a-box like Mei used to make for us. Drinks were passed around. Cars on the street above slowed down, people gawked at us foreigners lying around on rocks, barefoot and wet, with our shoes and socks and lunch boxes strewn everywhere.

Mei giggled and cried out, "All around me are *henna gaijin!* Strange foreigners. Help!"

Soaked to the skin, Marcus, Rob, and I dropped down to eat our *bentous.* We overheard Mei asking Reece, "This baptism, does it happen in a church?"

Feeding herself with chopsticks like a pro, Reece answered, "You can be baptized anywhere there's water."

Mei looked down the stream. "Even there?"

Reece's eyes lit up. "Totally."

"You must have a priest or minister?"

Marcus said, "Yeah, a priest. But you're lookin' at one."

Rob screwed up his face at Marcus. "Oh brother!"

Marcus tossed his head casually. "No joke, Shinobu. We're priests. You too—hard as that is to believe." Full of the same giddiness we were all feeling, Marcus stretched out on a big flat boulder and cried to the sky, "A holy nation called out of darkness into light. 'Once you were not a people, but now you are the people of God.'" He thrust a lazy fist to the sky, "My people!"

Mei said to us, "I want the baptism too."

I scouted out a deep, quiet pool downstream, and in a few minutes all of us had gathered. Dr. Dale did the honors of baptizing Mei. Everyone clapped and sang while cars on the highway slowed and people stared. Reece and Mei hugged and cried to each other, "My sister! My new sister!"

Jet lag—and what Dr. Eloise called spiritual fatigue—hit us like a strong drug. Back in our rooms we slept like logs. Next thing I knew it was dinnertime; our days and nights were all screwed up. We joined the SOS—and several more new faces—at a restaurant where you cook your own meal on a grill at your table. The specialty was *okonomiyaki,* a sort of big pancake with vegetables and any kind of meat you want to throw in. Reece and I sat with the Stallards and the SOS kids we'd hung out with at the shrine, Li and Robin.

While everyone was dumping ingredients onto their pancake batter and letting it grill, Dr. Eloise said to me, "Elijah, we told your mother that there was more to your ancestry than we had time to discuss. It's quite fascinating if you want to hear it. . . ."

"Shoot," I said.

"You do have Native American roots, but you are more heavily and originally Basque."

"Basque? What's that mean?"

Dr. Dale explained, "They are a unique people group who have occupied an area in western Europe for millennia. As we traced your lineage from the Isle of Magdeline further and further back in time, we discovered that Scottish and western Irish genetics are very similar to Basque."

I looked blank.

"We find it fascinating that your ancestors on both sides are the oldest and most intact people group known. Since the Upper Paleolithic era, they have occupied parts of France, Spain, and North Africa."

Rob, my history buff cousin, would find this interesting. But for some reason, only food and spending time with Reece were on my mind.

Dr. Elise said dramatically, "Before Rome became a world power, before the Goths invaded Europe, those called Basque had claimed a place in the world. And Mei will find this very intriguing—you must remember to tell her—there are striking linguistic similarities between the Basques and Mei's ancestors, the *Ainu.*"

Li jumped in and explained to Reece, "They're like the Indians of Japan."

"The word *ain'u* is an abbreviated Basque word meaning 'scattered or disappeared.' Your and Mei's people were probably forced apart due to a severe climate change: an ice age or famine. Mei's clan migrated east across the entire area that's now The Window and settled in the islands of Japan. Your clan moved north into the British Isles."

"I'm related to Mei?" I asked.

"Veeeerrry distantly," Dr. Eloise joked, then said to Li and Robin, "We've been wondering if he is the third Elijah and, therefore, interested in everything about him. We're archaeologists; we dig down."

Robin suddenly stopped cooking her pancake and gaped across the table at me. "The third Elijah? *You're the third Elijah!?*"

Li's narrow eyes popped. "The one who'll preach on the streets of Jerusalem at the end of days? Drama!"

Dr. Eloise put up a corrective hand. "There's no way to know until the time, dears. But we discovered another curiosity . . . oh, my pancake needs flipping. There . . . easy . . . ah, perfect! Now where was I?"

"The third Elijah," I reminded her. "I wondered about that when I was stuck in Gilead." (I didn't mention that I'd bargained with God to get me out of Gilead alive, even if it meant dying in a foreign country later—I was buying time.)

"Here's the surprise. Elijah, you are from Magdeline, Ohio—no news there. Your grandmother spent her days on the Isle of Magdeline—common knowledge now. But this prehistoric culture to which you can be traced is called . . ." She leaned in over her steaming pancake, "Magdelinian. By startling coincidence, you are connected to that name since the dawn of mankind."

My pancake looked done. I scooped it onto my plate and poured on the "bulldog sauce."(I was pretty sure it wasn't made from bulldogs; it smelled like barbecue sauce.) I tried not to get creeped out at the Stallards' poking into my history and bringing up all sorts of weird details. "What's that mean?"

In her usual flippant way, Dr. Eloise said, "Only God knows! But it is very curious indeed, isn't it? Three times over, you are a Magdelinian!"

"Like Mary Magdalene in the Bible?" Reece asked.

Dr. Dale refilled our teacups and smiled at me. "The woman from whom Jesus extracted seven demons? Slightly different spelling and no traceable genetic connection to our Magdelinian. But, yes—"

An explosion of cackles came from across the restaurant. Rob was making little hats for the fish heads at his table.

I had my Quella and looked up *Mary Magdalene.* "It says she was from Magdala on the southwest coast of the Sea of Galilee. Jesus cast seven demons out of her. She was one of a few devoted followers at the time of his death . . . the first to see him alive after the resurrection."

Dr. Eloise said, "Having been a captive of the dark side and come face-to-face with the Son of Light—to see him risen from the dead—I suppose one would be entirely devoted!" She pointed at my Quella with her chopstick. "There you have Mary Magdalene's entire history. But what a great lesson we have from her life: anyone can be snatched from the very gates of Hell."

"How did she get the demons?" Robin asked.

"Dabbling in the occult, most assuredly—like Elijah's forefathers, the MacMerrits; opening the forbidden doors; parting that veil between the worlds."

Dr. Dale shook his head. "It was your former path, Elijah. Your openness to the spirit world without guidance from the Word, ancestors immersing themselves in the occult, your parents' own disinterest in the things of God . . ." His eyes drifted out the dark window. "Your chances for ever meeting him were slim indeed."

"Slim to none, without me!" Reece nudged me, grinning.

I thought of how I'd always believed in a Great Spirit of some kind without understanding anything about him. How I'd wanted to visit the Crystal See even when the minister preached against it. How much I'd wanted to see the dark side when I was in Ireland. "So what does it mean that I'm a . . . Magdelinian?" I asked.

Dr. Dale chuckled heartily. "Apparently, it's up to you to find out, Elijah."

Chapter 8

AFTER dinner we walked to a community center a few blocks away on a side street. On the second floor was a big Japanese-style room with paper screens and tatami mat floors. We took off our shoes and sat on big square pillows.

Dr. Eloise padded over to me in bare feet. "We will show the armor tonight. Would you like to model it?"

I looked around at the crowd. "Um, I'll pass."

There were over two hundred people there, way fewer than I expected for a global conference, but people from all over: Baruti from Egypt, Paulo and Ramona from Brazil, the Bremmer family from Switzerland, and so on.

Dr. Dale put up the map he'd spread open at Gilead, showing The Window. After announcements and prayers for the world, we sang a bunch of songs. There was a guitar and bongos and a flute player sometimes. A guy named Fred played banjo. Not all the songs were in English, but nobody seemed to care; they hummed when they didn't know the words. I was trying to figure out the purpose of the conference when Dr. Dale asked my clan to stand so he could introduce us. Turns out that we were the visual presentation for an hour lecture. (The whole time we were up there, I knew they'd want to see the Tear of Blood before the night was over. The pancake with bulldog sauce lay in my stomach like a rock.)

Dr. Dale began the introductions with Reece, describing her has having "extraordinary spiritual vitality," that she was "quite unsinkable." He explained in clinical terms why she had to use a crutch. "Unfortunately, even with current medical technology, there is little hope she will completely recover. But that does not stop her!"

He went on. "Mei Aizawa is a new believer. She acclimates well to changing surroundings, is gifted artistically, highly intelligent, cooperative—an excellent team member. She has lived in the States and visited the British Isles, is willing to work alone if necessary. Mei is quite the brave one. And after only a few years in the States, she was in the ninety-five percentile range for language comprehension!"

People clapped. Rob was next in line. He stepped forward stiffly and beamed. It sort of felt like we were beauty contestants without a runway.

Marcus barked, "Go, Shinobu!"

Dr. Dale said officially, "Rob Wingate is the whimsical one, if you haven't guessed," Twitters went around the audience. "He is naturally curious, a researcher, a detail man. Good navigator. Rob stood up to his father during a family crisis and single-handedly turned the situation around."

A few oohs and aahs. Rob's eyes shifted shyly to us. He murmured, "I had help."

"And Marcus," Dr. Dale said warmly. "Street-smart and charming. An excellent fact finder. He's familiar with diverse cultures, comes from excellent parental stock.

Marcus would make a good detective, I think. Just enough intimidation in his manner to get information when needed."

Excellent *stock?!* Now I was feeling like one of Morgan's prize bulls up for auction. I caught Marcus's eye and brainwaved, *What gives?*

He shrugged, caught Karinna's admiring eye in the audience, and winked.

I whispered to him out of the corner of my mouth, "Do the words *Miranda Varner* ring a bell?"

Dr. Dale stepped over to me. "And finally, Elijah Creek. Emotionally and physically tough. You must hear his story about surviving six days in freezing temperatures, trapped under an enormous rock—without food, water, or shelter." (More oohs and aahs.) "Elijah has received a clear call from the Almighty, has demonstrated the gift of discernment, and has encountered one of the dark forces while in Ireland."

My clan looked at me questioningly.

Dr. Dale went on, "And it is through Elijah and his friends that we are able to make the next presentation."

The lights dimmed. Dr. Eloise and a dummy covered with a white sheet appeared in the back corner of the room from behind a paper screen. One small ceiling light beamed down on Dr. Eloise's ghostly sidekick. She announced loudly, "The Magdeline children—" (I wondered if she'd still be calling us children when we were in our fifties and she was a hundred.) "—found the armor of God, which" (she adjusted the ghost to face the crowd) "we have brought for everyone to see! Some scoff at the armor of God, its power and protection. Skeptics have doubted its existence, called it a mere metaphor, but . . ."

The flute and drum began a mysterious tune—haunting and tribal-sounding. Dramatically, Dr. Eloise threw the sheet off with a *whoosh*. The crowd gasped. There, for the first time in ages, stood the whole armor of God with all of the pieces—including the sword—gleaming in the spotlight on a dummy wrapped in black, like Rob had done in his attic.

Everyone applauded.

Then the armor moved.

Another gasp went up from the crowed. A couple of girls screamed. A real person was wearing the armor! Nervous giggles followed, but the effect was pretty awesome. Slowly, silently, the armor floated through the crowd, pantomiming a battle, lifting the shield of faith against invisible projectiles, thrusting the sword into unseen enemies. Light flashed off the helmet and sword; the black-clad arms and legs and face practically disappeared. It moved to the rhythm of the drum as smooth and liquid as the flute melody.

I scanned the crowd to see who was missing, who was wearing the armor.

Marcus leaned over and whispered, "Dmitri."

I nodded agreement. The dark warrior matched Dmitri's muscular build.

The Stallards had made their big splash. The lights came

up, and for the next half hour people swarmed around the armor, touching it ever so carefully. The old archaeologists had the time of their lives showing how each piece was created from fragments of history: from the Viking torq around the neck to the scraps of the tabernacle lining the breastplate; from the *Ogham* inscription of faith on the shield to the worn sandals of ancient mariners sailing from Europe to America and back.

The Stallards had us sit up front, like a panel. Mei was asked to tell how she and Rob had found the Chinese letter hidden in the breastplate, how the symbol for *righteousness* means "lamb over me." Reece explained that finding the belt of truth had uncovered one of Magdeline's darkest lies. Marcus demonstrated how word-searching the Quella led us to a burning car where the shield of faith was stashed. The SOS kids grumbled; they wanted Quellas too.

I told how even when I was trapped in Gilead, God had told me in code where to find the helmet of salvation, which I'd lost the year before.

The armor-clad phantom went back to the corner and stood like a castle guard under the spotlight. Dr. Dale summed up, "Friends, we have gathered here to retreat from the battle this week. We will share our stories, salve our wounds, rearm and reconnect with our God, our source of strength. He created this armor as surely as he made the spiritual armor we wear. These pieces were crafted across continents and through millennia from the histories of true warriors: worshipers in the Holy Land, pilgrims who died alone and lie in unmarked graves, spiritual wanderers venturing into the unknown to serve him. Nameless heroes lost in jungles and locked in dungeons.

"These precious pieces of leather and metal armor—like God's real armor—have been stashed away unused for too long. We shall not be able to show our amazing relic to the world for it to be dismembered and disputed over. But no matter. The full armor of God is not a relic; it is a reality."

During a coffee break, the SOS hung out with us. We kicked back and relaxed. But the knot in my stomach jumped to my throat when Dr. Eloise came over. "Elijah, when we reconvene, might we have a look at the Tear of Blood? It will be a moment they will never forget!"

The audience sat down with hot drinks and smiles of anticipation. I stood, let out a long, slow breath and began. I told them about finding the red diamond in the helmet of salvation, how I'd assumed it was glass and spilled the beans to New York Jewelers, how in a few weeks' time, news had reached around the globe. And how that made me a marked man. Though I'd passed myself off as George Telanoo from Georgia, I still feared that roughly half the human population was ready to slit my throat to have the diamond.

The Stallards sat there beaming. They thought I was leading up to big drama like they had done. My heart pounded in my ears. "If that armor of God is a symbol of spiritual things," I pointed to the pieces now spread out neatly in the corner, "then so is the Tear of Blood. I've been thinking about its purpose for over a year. It was in the helmet of salvation, so its message has to be about saving people. I think it stands for God's tears over his lost children and the drops of blood Jesus gave. The triangle facets stand for Father, Son, and Holy Spirit. Mind, body, and spirit. Birth, death, resurrection. Yesterday, today, forever . . . a hundred meanings."

I cleared my throat. My face felt hot. "But instead of a great treasure, it ended up being a burden, heavier than that two-ton rock in Gilead. It was only a matter of time before I'd be found, my family would be robbed or kidnapped, and it would be lost forever. My family, they're not believers yet. How could I risk their lives over a rock? Yeah, I know it's priceless and forged from fires in the bowels of the earth and all that . . . I lost a week's sleep deciding what to do with it."

The Stallards turned somber. Their backs went stiff.

"After Gilead, and after I'd preached to my high school, a new kind of fearlessness came over me. But at the same time, I was going back into fear because of the diamond. I couldn't walk down Main Street for thinking I'd be mugged. God wouldn't want me living like that."

The smiles completely faded from the Stallards' faces. They knew something was up.

Pulling four velvet pouches out of my jacket pocket, I heaved a breath. "Well, this is as good a time as any." I handed out the pouches to my clan. When they poured out their jewelry, it took a moment to register what I'd done with the Tear of Blood. Every kind of expression washed across their faces: shock, excitement, disbelief, anger.

"I had to," I looked at the baffled audience. "I had to."

I said to the clan, "I had the Tear of Blood divided. I designed the jewelry like I thought you'd want. Mei, yours is a pendant that looks like a compass. Wherever you go, God will guide you.

"Rob, yours is a ring. The spiral design is the whirlwind that wrecked your house but worked things out with your family for the best. Marcus, yours is an ID bracelet. The stone is in a sand dollar design, which tells the story of Jesus. You can have anything you want engraved on the bracelet. Reece, the last piece broke in two when the gem master was working on it, so I had it made into earrings. They're eagle feathers. You know what they mean."

I explained how I'd used the sixth cut for payment. "The metal is electrum—gold and silver—like Job 22:25-28 says: 'The Almighty will be your gold, the choicest silver for you.' We'd looked at this verse, but never read the rest. Get this: 'Surely then you will find delight in the Almighty and will lift up your face to God. You will pray to him, and he will hear you, and you will fulfill your vows. What you decide on will be done, and light will shine on your ways.'"

I looked at the Stallards pleadingly. Their expressions were blank with shock. "If we think this diamond was

valuable, just think how much power is in every drop of
God's blood, how much his tears cost: enough to save
millions of people in every single drop. I couldn't hide it
away, Dr. Dale! I couldn't be on the run the rest of my life
because of a priceless piece of rock. *It's just a rock!* All the
world wants it, but the world doesn't understand what
it's really worth—what it really means. The Tear of Blood
isn't for a museum or some filthy-rich woman to wear at
big parties. It's supposed to help truth go out to the whole
world before the Day of Evil comes. It's about salvation."

I looked back to my clan. "You each have a piece of the
Tear of Blood. You have a job to do, a vow to fulfill. If you
don't want to do it, pass along your treasure."

Marcus fastened the heavy bracelet around his wrist and
got choked up. "Thanks, man. Thanks."

As the others put their jewelry on, I finished up. "If the
Day of Evil comes and you need to sell it for food or to help
people, do it. Don't feel bad. I don't know how much the
jewelry is worth, but it's a lot."

"Where's yours?" Reece whispered.

I grinned. "I'm not much for jewelry."

She looked horrified, "You don't have one?"

"Yeah, I do."

She reached over, tugged on my earlobe, and frowned.
"Where is it?"

I yanked the waistband of my khakis down and showed
them my belly button.

Rob guffawed. "You had it pierced?!"

I looked over the crowd. "If anyone wants mine, if you need it right now, it's yours."

For a minute there was dead silence. People glanced around uneasily to see how other people were reacting. Then Dr. Dale pulled his old, arthritic self up off his floor cushion and limped over to me. Deliberately he put his hand in mine. "Wisdom," he said deeply. He raised his other hand to Heaven. "'I praise you, Father, Lord of heaven and earth, because you have hidden these things from the wise and learned, and revealed them to little children.'" Then he put his hands together. One clap, then two, then another. Slowly everyone in the room stood and clapped and smiled at us. Waves of relief washed over me. The old scientist nodded to the crowd. "'The price of wisdom is beyond rubies.'"

I realized in that moment how much the Stallards' respect meant to me.

Dr. Dale and Dr. Eloise admitted they were shocked but applauded my "uncommonly clear perspective." Whatever. I was just glad not to be clobbered for committing some crime of global proportions.

The clan was all over me with thanks, saying how they liked the jewelry and how they'd honor its purpose. Then Reece nailed me. She got right up under my nose and demanded, "Okay. What's this about the dark forces? Spill!"

Chapter 9

MY clan was on a huge high. We'd stormed the gates without a scratch, had a great meal (Rob renamed it okeydokey-yaki because he liked the taste but couldn't say the word). We'd shown off the armor of God to people from all over the world. The Stallards were pretty okay with my breaking up the Tear of Blood into pieces—huge relief. So we five wanted to go out on the town, even though there wasn't much town to go out on. While the Stallards were in meetings, we went to the *ofuro* and then called the SOS to come over. While we hung out in the girls' room to wait, I explained about the dark forces, how in that bookstore in Ireland the clerk had said in a demon voice, "You'll never find it," and how it rattled me—especially after our futile search for the sword. The clan was stone sober taking it in. Even Marcus, who'd bragged about his knowledge of the dark side . . . stunned speechless.

Finally, Rob said in a creeped-out way, "You mean . . . demons are really real?"

"But God's more real," Reece said earnestly.

Marcus looked at me curiously. "Something my dad said, Takumi, about your needing spiritual backup . . . you told him about this, didn't you?"

"I had to get it off my chest. But we did find the sword though, so the evil voice was lying."

Reece said doubtfully, "We haven't found the word on it."

"We will," I insisted. "It's got to be there."

The SOS came over with dripping hair and dressed in blue *yukatas,* just like us, and for a second I imagined them all as my clan. We strolled through the village, sporting our new jewelry, dodging sidewalk bicyclists every few minutes. Nothing was open but bars, so we found a bunch of vending machines and dug out pocket change for royal milk tea. Mei was our resident expert, and people kept asking her what foods were good. Li worked his way over to her and said, *"Moukari makka?"*

Beaming with surprise, she went all coy and answered, *"Bochibochi denna."* She translated for us. "He said, 'How's business?' and I said, 'So-so.' He speaks my Osaka dialect!"

Mei and Li went off in their own little world, using a bunch of languages. I couldn't read Marcus, but he sure kept an eye on them, at least until Karinna and her friends swarmed him.

We strolled along in the warm evening breeze. A starry sky spread over the looming black mountains. From what Reece and I picked up, the Students of the Seven Seas were kids with an interest in global spiritual problems. Some had parents in the same business; others had to go to church alone or in secret. Mahesh was kicked out of his family for his beliefs and wasn't sure where he'd go after his SOS tour of duty was over.

It wasn't long before Rob was goofing off doing his Ohio

version of a ninja. Even if he'd had the traditional black getup, he'd have looked goofy enough. But a block away, dancing around Marcus in his long tight robe, chopping the air, he was an old, bald lady fighting off a nonchalant mugger. Reece giggled, "They're at it again. Will it never end?"

Their stark silhouettes highlighted by streetlights, Rob thrust stiff hands in front of Marcus and cried, "AaeeeeeAH!"

Marcus eased back and said coolly (to impress Karinna), "Don't want to hurt you, buddy." Rob froze for a second, then whirled around and skittered with baby steps across the street.

Reece asked, "Where's he going?"

"Running start. He's getting steam for a karate kick at Marcus . . . but . . . oh no . . . no, Rob! Wait! Your skirt!"

Hands in a chop-chop position, he loped sideways across the street toward Marcus, hollering, "Aaeeeah-HYA!" and kicked. That *yukata* bound him up below the knees; his left leg shot out, the other leg came up with it, and he went sailing sideways in midair, like a cartoon. Marcus eased out of the way, and Rob disappeared into an alley—followed by an awful racket of trash cans, bikes, and who-knows-what echoing down the street.

Eva from Germany ran into the alley to retrieve the body of my crazy cousin; the rest of the SOS lost it. They hung off each other clutching their stomachs; they leaned against street poles in hysterics. One guy dropped to the street on his knees and howled like a coyote. In a minute Rob emerged to the wild applause of the SOS and made a deep curtsy.

Reece hugged my arm. "I'm so glad he's one of us."

"'Lijah!"

My head jerked off the pillow, the urgent whisper jarring me awake. The room was pitch-black. "What time is it?"

"'Lijah, pretend you're asleep!" Rob wheezed.

"I *was* asleep!" I moaned and dropped back on the pillow.

"I know, but pretend you are!" Frantically he piled pillows and clothes on his pallet, covering them with a blanket until it looked like a body asleep. He jumped over me onto Marcus's pallet. Marcus wasn't there. "Restroom," Rob explained. Hurriedly he hid himself under a pile of dirty laundry beside Marcus's backpack.

Retribution, I thought and snickered, "Got it."

"Shhh!"

Turning toward Marcus's pallet, I pulled my covers around my face, closed my eyes, and waited for the show to start.

The door clicked open; feet padded on straw mat. I adjusted my breathing, slow and regular. He plopped down on the pallet . . . a rustle of sheets, then all quiet. My eyes opened to slits, and because I'd trained myself to see in the dark, I could make out his profile. For a few minutes, it was quiet except for steady breathing. I bit my lip with anticipation. Then from the other side of Marcus came a low, guttural, "Mmaarrccuuss . . ."

Half awake, Marcus wailed like a siren with weak batteries, "OooooooowhatISIT!?" He came straight up off the floor like he'd been detonated, and flung himself over me. Landing on Rob's squishy fake body, he made a sick cat sound of disgust. To keep him from hurtling through the paper screen, I grabbed his arm; he thought the thing had him and squealed like a girl.

Rob exploded from the pile of dirty laundry, raised his fists, and cried victoriously, "I am Shinobu! Master of Stealth!!"

Once we'd peeled Marcus off the ceiling, we lay there in the dark, too wired to sleep. Ryo, the "cool" one, had blown his cover. In the end he didn't really mind the prank: "Shinobu, you'll always get the last laugh. You're a dangerous man."

It seemed like life couldn't get any better, like nothing could ever go wrong.

The next morning the SOS joined us on the busy sidewalk outside the inn. The day was already heating up. The Stallards came down in matching brown suits. Rob couldn't wait to tell everyone how Marcus "went soprano" on him last night. In talkative clumps, we made a left and headed into town, dodging oncoming bicyclists.

Dr. Eloise said, "Careful there, Reece, watch those tricky holes in the sidewalk. Now where is that bakery I noticed yesterday? Ah, across the street. And some of our people. *Ohayou!* Good morning!" She waved and then chirped, "Dale, assist Reece if you will."

We started crossing the busy street a few at a time. Dr. Dale took Reece's arm. She smiled and sang, "To the left, to the left, to the left left left."

Dodging traffic, Rob and Marcus danced across, trading karate moves. Mei was looking up, explaining a road sign to Eva. Reece was right in front of me. It happened so fast, I didn't see it coming. There was nothing I could have done.

Chapter 10

A sickening thud. A horrible, hurtling black blur.
Shattering glass. A heavy crunch shook the ground. The car
didn't even slow down. It plowed right into our group. Dr.
Eloise fell back. Her arm shot out in front of Reece, who
stumbled back into me. Dr. Dale, who'd been standing at
right angles to Reece and guiding her steps, took a direct
hit and disappeared. He was there, and then he wasn't.
Screams. Tires squealed. Other cars screeched to a stop. Cries
of horror. The hiss of air: blown tires, engine steam. A razor-
sharp flashback cut through my mind: the grill of the black
coupe had slammed into his legs, his shoulder hit the hood,
he went into the windshield, it shattered, the car careened
full force into a utility pole. *God* . . . A quiet voice that was
mine came from a deep place inside me, a knowing place. I
was already past wishing *no, please no*. It had happened in the
blink of an eye. There was nothing anyone could have done.

Reece was chalk white, her eyes glazed and confused. I
put my arm around her, scanned the crowd to locate the
guys, and ordered them back across the street. "Marcus!
Come on, but watch out! Rob, you too!" Then Mei had
hold of Reece. The guys dashed across the stalled traffic and
stared in horror at the car. I stepped into their sight line.
"He's gone. Take the SOS and Reece and go back to the inn

. . . unless anyone saw the whole thing—they should stay. I'll need Mei here. Reece, go with the others." Adults from the conference were running toward us. "Anybody else here speak Japanese?" I asked them.

Li was there. "I know a little."

"Right. Hang close." I'd gone into camp counselor mode without realizing it. Where was Dr. Eloise? There, at the crushed, steaming car. I went over to her. The whole front of the black coupe had collapsed on impact, Dr. Dale thrown into the front seat. He was curled up, his face pressed against the back of the seat. As if he'd fallen asleep in the car. Peaceful, still. Dr. Eloise reached her hand into the car's shattered side window and patted the familiar brown suit, now covered with pebbles of broken glass. *No blood. Not a drop. Probably didn't want to inconvenience anyone*, I thought with a strange, crazy detachment. *Didn't want to be any trouble*. I put a hand on Dr. Eloise's shoulder.

Eventually she looked up at me, her eyes glittering with tears, her thin lips quivering. "It was painless, wasn't it?"

"Yeah. It was."

She kept patting his back. "He never did relish the thought of lingering . . . some long, slow disease . . . he never wanted that. . . . He didn't even feel it."

"Not a thing. Why don't you go to that step and sit down?" I suggested. "The police will be here soon."

She didn't hear me but leaned further into the car, reaching over her husband to the man slumped over the steering wheel, motionless. "Oh dear," she said sadly. "Oh dear, sweet man! Lord, take his spirit if you will. He didn't know what he was doing. I'm sure he didn't know." She touched his head as if to give him a blessing, then straightened up and sniffled. "Sit where? Over there by the little garden? Don't the Japanese do wonders with their small spaces? Thank you, Elijah. Are the others all right?"

"We're good. You should sit down."

People from the conference encircled her. I edged myself out and found Mei. Crying but calm, she explained what would happen when the police came. It was pretty much the same as in the States. They'd want to talk to every witness. (But since Reece didn't see a thing, what good would it do for her to be here? I'd seen the look on her face. I knew, probably better than she did, what she was thinking.) Others had seen the fatal black car run a red light and swerve for half a block, not once putting on the brakes. Mei said drunk driving was a big problem in her culture. "In America too," I said.

The conference people stood around sniffling, lips moving. While the police took statements, I weaved through the crowd, dazed but alert. They were crying and thanking God for the accident in the same breath, asking him to use it. To use them. To shine through the loss. They might have been speaking in a foreign language, it seemed so strange to me. Why weren't they bawling and asking why, why, why?

For a moment I stood there in a haze, remembering three years ago when Reece had first mentioned God using you. The idea had really turned me off. Getting used had seemed like a lame way to live. I looked around at the group, a hundred calm, sad people wearing their peace and faith . . . like armor. Getting used by God was Dr. Dale's reason for being. Theirs too. Yesterday they'd used words as weapons, now for comfort. Random thoughts floated through my head. *Dr. Dale's gone. He went down inches from us. We were inches from death. Reece. Inches. Like on the Cliffs of Morte . . . like me in Gilead . . . Dr. Dale was here. Now he's . . . somewhere in eternity.*

A kind of quiet bubble surrounded me, and it seemed I heard his old, gentle voice say, *"The walls between the worlds are always thin, Elijah. Always thin."*

Reports were filed, two bodies taken away. Traffic was diverted to let the tow truck through. A crowd of hushed villagers milled around, not caring if they were late for work. My clan and the SOS wandered back out. As the car was being hauled off, a youngish Japanese woman came running down the middle of the street, her apron flying, her house slippers flapping, a look of terrified expectation on her face. One glance at the car and she stopped and crumpled to the street.

I didn't need an English translation to understand what was happening: the drunk man was her husband. A woman storekeeper came into the street and knelt down to comfort her; the wife asked how it happened; the storekeeper explained. Then the storekeeper nodded to Dr. Eloise who had stepped to the curb. The young Japanese wife got up, her face frozen in shame and fear; her husband had killed that foreign woman's husband.

Dr. Eloise stepped into the street, and the two women locked eyes. The wife stepped back, bracing for the foreigner's rage. The whole town stood still. Dr. Eloise stretched out her arms and called out, *"Daijoubu!* It's all right!" The wife stiffened as Dr. Eloise grasped her shoulders, looked into her face, and said, *"Daijoubu,* my friend!" Alone in a huge circle of onlookers, the widows clung to each other and cried and cried.

News spread among the conference people that regular meetings were postponed until further notice. There'd be a get-together tonight, a cremation in the morning.

All day Reece didn't come out of her room. She wouldn't talk to anyone or eat anything. Mei's face was strained and sad. As dinnertime approached, I knocked on their door. Mei opened it slightly. Over her head I saw Reece on her pallet, facing the wall.

Mei stepped into the hall and whispered, "She thinks it was her fault because she was joking to Dr. Dale about 'to the left left left,' and he was supposed to look to the right. The cars come from the right."

"Reece?" I called into her room.

"Go away."

"Reece, come on—"

"Go away!"

Chapter 11

WE gathered in the meeting room at the community center. Fred played his banjo, easy and gentle and full of hope. People hovered around Dr. Eloise like guardian angels; they sat at her feet like children. We four sank down in a corner watching like outsiders for a while, with nothing much to say until Veronica came over. "How are you kids holding up?"

"We're okay," I said halfheartedly. "Reece is back at the inn. She's tired."

She sat down next to me. "I came to say thanks, Elijah."

"For what?"

She chuckled. "You took over. You started handling things seconds before the rest of us—adults included—registered what had even happened."

I shrugged. "I was right there."

"You have amazing presence of mind in a crisis," she said, studying me.

"My dad owns a nature camp. I help him a lot because there's always something."

She agreed, "Yes, there's always something, isn't there? Sounds like you have lots of experience."

The evening wore on. Food was brought, floor cushions handed out. Blankets came and Dr. Eloise rested. I worried about Reece. Then who should walk in with a woman at his side but Donovan.

Mahesh said, "Look, it's Donovan and Hester."

I knew without asking that the woman was the daughter of Dale and Eloise. Hester was every bit a Stallard, just thirty years younger: slight build, energetic, bright eyes, short brown hair, and clothes so old-fashioned they were cool again. They hugged and cried with Dr. Eloise; then Donovan came over. We all stood and shook hands.

"How's that foot?" Donovan asked.

"Good."

He looked us over and asked kindly, "How's everyone doing?"

"Okay. Reece is sleeping."

He nodded toward Dr. Eloise. "I need to get back to the family. We'll talk later."

Mahesh leaned over, amazed. "You know them already?"

"Yeah."

"Wow. They're *parabolani*," he said.

I must have looked blank.

"They didn't tell you?"

Now I felt really stupid. "No."

"They will, I guess. Once you're in."

When we sat down again, I looked to Rob, the smart one. *"Parabo . . . ?"*

Marcus had a strange look on his face. "Mom and Dad have used that word. I thought it was spy stuff."

When the swarm of people cleared around Dr. Eloise, she caught sight of us in the corner and came over—her eyes red-rimmed, a strong smile on her face. "We are not going home, children. He wouldn't have wanted that. After the cremation, I will need to tie up a few loose ends here. I'll join you in Shimabara. But I'm afraid you will have to do the prayer journey at Mei's on your own. Are you prepared?"

"We can handle it," I said confidently. "Same as at Nikko."

No one wanted to leave the meeting room. It was looking like an all-nighter, so I slipped out and went back to the inn. I knocked on Reece's door.

"Go away."

I went in anyway and sat beside her on the floor. She knew I was there but didn't say anything. After a long while, I said, "Reece, get up." She ignored me. I waited a few minutes then barked, "I said get up!"

Startled by my harsh tone, she sat up and wobbled but wouldn't look at me, her eyes cast down, hair hanging over her face. I pulled her to me and hugged her hard. "You didn't do it, Reece! It wasn't your fault."

She leaned against me lifelessly and whimpered, "I said, 'to the left,' and he looked left. He didn't look to the right. I knew he always got it confused, but I was joking around."

"He was an old guy," I said nonchalantly. "He wasn't going to last much longer anyway. And Dr. Eloise said he would have wanted to go that way. It was better for him than to have a lingering disease and suffer a lot."

She was limp as a dishrag in my arms. Wouldn't say a word. Where was the feisty, optimistic, outspoken, unsinkable Reece Elliston? Where had she gone? I wondered if I'd lost two people.

The next morning I went by the girls' room. Mei came out alone and closed the door. "She is so sad she can't lift up her head."

"You guys go on. I'll catch up."

I went in, knelt down beside her, and grabbed her shoulders. "Reece, look at me!" She wouldn't. I made her sit up. "Hey, girl, if you believe anything that you yourself have told me over the past three years, then Dr. Dale is in Heaven and having the time of his life. If you don't believe that—if you've been making all this up—then you're a big fat liar, and you need to go home!"

Her eyes drifted up to me. She was hardly breathing. "He died because he was helping me."

"No, Reece, he died because he got hit by a drunk driver. It happens every day in every country in the world. Come on, this isn't like you. It was horrible, but we gotta get a grip, okay?" I brushed the hair out of her face. "Hey, there's a world out there that needs protecting, and we have the whole armor of God, remember? That's why we're here. I'm not leaving without you. Remember what I always say? It's our motto: if I'm going, you're going."

Donovan's memorial speech gave details of Dr. Dale's life I never knew. He was born and raised in Nebraska, lost his parents young, served in the military, had degrees in history, archaeology, and anthropology. Married at twenty-one, he had one daughter, Hester. "Dale Stallard made significant discoveries in the field of Near Eastern studies before his life purpose changed course. My father-in-law was an atheist until he began to compare the ancient history he knew so well with the Word of the living God. He found that Word to be true. More than true. Dad discovered it was *the* truth."

He paused and looked around at the crowd sitting informally on cushions. "A friend of mind once said that each person you meet comes into your life with an encrypted message from God. So instead of me rambling, I'd like anyone who knew Dale Stallard to briefly tell the message you received from him."

Dozens of adults took turns saying stuff about his radical faith, his quiet courage, about times when they were ready to give up and then Dale and Eloise showed up out of nowhere and talked them through it. Then Donovan nodded to me. My clan stood together.

Choking back tears, Reece started, "I'll . . . I'll always remember how he fought for us in prayer. And how he died helping me."

Dr. Eloise said, "Reece, dear heart, it was his time, not yours. Don't grieve. He would gladly have gone in your place."

The room got quiet.

I spoke up. "When we were in Ireland and he quit eating, that's what I'll remember. He was worried about us and wondered why God had chosen a bunch of dumb kids to find his armor. But he didn't lecture or point out our faults. He took the burden on himself. I'll never forget how he helped me build a fire—" my voice cracked, "a fire on the Hill of Slane and how he read from the *Warrior* against the darkness that night."

Rob spoke up next. "I guess he taught me that it's cool to be a nerd, even an old one. So there's hope for me."

Everyone chuckled, and for a minute the sadness eased up.

Mei sniffled. "Our tradition in Japan is to honor the old ones. So I couldn't believe that Dr. Dale was happy to be my friend. He honored *me!* Dr. Stallard was a very honorable man."

Marcus stared at the floor, his jaw was clenched. He couldn't speak.

"Marcus," said Dr. Eloise, "it's all right."

"The last thing he said to me—" he turned away and swallowed hard. "After the day at the shrine up there, I was going off on how cool it was to be bringing down pagan gods with words. He said, 'Humble yourself before the Lord, Marcus, and he will lift you up. Don't exalt yourself. Let him raise you up.'" Marcus gulped hard, wiped his eyes. "I'll work on it."

Dr. Eloise called out, "Oh, how he believed in you

children! Dale called you his Magdeline Five. In like manner to the Cambridge Seven, those courageous young people of European history, journeying to the very ends of the earth! Why, just yesterday morning as we lay in the quiet of our room, he said to me, 'Eloise, God has not spared our Magdeline Five the pains of this life, but he has certainly called them out of their lives into his work. How fiercely he must love them!' He sat watching the morning come with a glorious smile on his face and said, 'Long after we're gone, God will use them.'"

My clan sat down. Except for sniffling and clearing of throats, it was quiet for a long time. Then Fred started playing his banjo again. Someone started singing. We joined in where we could—songs about Heaven, how God reigns there, and how the rhythm of his power echoes throughout the world. Guitar and bongos joined in. For a half hour, people sang in all kinds of languages. At the end there was a standing ovation to Dr. Dale and to the God he served. My throat was so tight I couldn't talk afterward.

Everyone was wrung out, but again no one could leave the community center. It started looking like a lock-in at church: people eating, some singing, playing cards, or sound asleep on pillows. Marcus called his dad to tell him the news; Dom Skidmore offered to bring us all home. We said we were fine, that we still had a prayer journey to make. He promised to call our parents and tell them the sad news.

Some of the SOS kids came over and wanted to know

more about us being the Magdeline Five. As we went around the circle reliving the past three years, I myself was shocked, even though I'd lived it. Rob told about his parents almost splitting up, how he'd almost drowned on Farr Island, how a tornado slammed his house. Reece told how she went down at Hermits' Cave looking for the shoes of peace, and how God had taken away her pain the night of her operation. I explained how the quest had led us to the grave of Kate Dowland and stirred up the whole town and uncovered why Old Pilgrim Church had died. It was great to talk about it openly after so long. No secrets.

While Marcus was telling about how his parents' friendship with the Stallards had got us connected in the first place, Mahesh started looking at him weird. "Your dad knows the Stallards?"

"Yeah. They met in the Middle East."

"Is he part of the network?"

Marcus said uncertainly, "He knows about it."

Mahesh asked at the others, "Doesn't Marcus look a lot like Metatron?"

Through that night—in a foreign country, at the foot of a mountain ruled by pagan gods, with that dream of the threatening flower at the front of my mind, and having lost our adopted grandpa—in all that strangeness, the Magdeline Five learned some surprising facts. Number one: Dom—aka Metatron—and Donovan were *parabolani*.

Sitting cross-legged with a cup of coffee in his hands, Donovan explained it this way: "In the early days of the church, there came to be a group of people who rescued fellow Christians in danger and retrieved the bodies of those lost in spiritual warfare. They were the *parabolani*, the riskers, who gambled with their lives to help others. Today they do everything from smuggling Bibles to outfitting and equipping missionaries."

Li added, "Some are experts in security systems and high-tech communications."

Rob interrupted, "Like Dr. Eloise's binoculars with a secret recording device?"

Mahesh said, "And escape techniques, like jumping out of buildings blindfolded."

Karinna added, "They have hiding places all over the world for when the Day of Evil comes."

"Dunluce Castle was one!" Reece cried. "The Stallards were starting to show us!"

Li said, "My country has thousands of places. I even know a few."

I said to Donovan, "So when you and Dom rescued me, you were being the . . . the *para*—?"

"*Parabolani*. We prayed for rescue . . . and thank God for that little fire you set."

I winked at Reece, remembering how I'd burned her poem. "Without that piece of paper I'd have had no fire."

Donovan said, "Without that fire you wouldn't be here.

You had two days left at the most. Now, the *peregrini:* these are pilgrims who move often and acclimate to other cultures quickly. At the first level of spiritual warfare, they pray at strongholds. Like you already saw. On the next level, they go into the dangerous places and preach the gospel in homes, churches, on street corners. The *peregrini* venture into hostile areas for short periods, do their work, and clear out to avoid capture. The apostle Paul is the model of a *peregrini.*"

"And Patrick of Ireland," I added, "and Columba and Brendan. Dr. Dale told us about the *peregrini*. And about seraphs."

He nodded. "Seraphs—the burning ones—are the third category: missionaries. We call them seraphs when we're in high-threat situations. These are preachers, teachers, and doctors who settle in a place for long periods of time—even for life. Theirs may be the least dangerous but the most lonely, difficult work. They stay because of a burning passion for the lost. No matter what, they stay."

Mahesh turned to Marcus. "I met your father once. He is *parabolani* and has no fear. Big and scary. Tough talker."

"Where? How?" Marcus looked miffed that a stranger could know more about his dad than he did.

Li said, "At orientation in Alaska. He told a story about a guy named Metatron going into a jungle to rescue a captured missionary. The missionary was cut loose and escaped. Metatron disappeared. Everybody was sure he was killed, until he showed up two weeks later—just walked out of the jungle hungry as a horse. Then your dad explained how he did it. He's a legend."

Rob gaped at me. "Farr Island, guys! Dom and his two buddies hiding in the trees, teaching us jungle warfare! He said it was a refresher course, to keep his reflexes on alert!"

"Saving the world," I muttered, dumbfounded. "When we visited that military base, Peck and Yancy said they had to get back to saving the world. They're *parabolani?*" I asked Donovan. "How big is this network?"

"Nobody knows because it's invisible." He grinned. "Well, God knows. But he's the only one. Commander in chief, you see. These three branches of the network form what we call the helix."

"People in churches—do they know?" I asked.

He shrugged. "Some of them get it. Some don't." Donovan excused himself and went back to Hester.

"So who is the SOS?" I asked Mahesh. "Are you guys seraphs or *peregrini* or *parabolani?*"

"We don't know who we are yet, or if we qualify. That's why we're SOS—basic training."

Leaning against the wall angrily, his green eyes hard as stone, Marcus demanded, "How many of you—ballpark figure?"

Li said, "Three hundred on our ship."

"Where are the rest?" Mei asked.

"All over Japan . . . working. We'll set sail again in September for survival training in Samoa. Don't ask me how many ships. I don't know. The inland teams are in the thousands, maybe millions. I'm not sure. But what about you Magdeline Five—are you joining?"

Dr. Dale was cremated the next day. Dr. Eloise invited us to go along with Donovan and Hester, Veronica, and a few other adults because, as she said, "You five were the closest to grandchildren he had."

His body was in a box with a glass lid. Flowers were around his face. Donovan said a prayer for us and for the Japanese woman who also lost her husband. Then a door in the wall opened and the casket slid into another room. We went down to a waiting area.

Dr. Eloise sat next to us. "Perhaps this is not the best time, children, but a decision must be made about the armor. Now that its existence has been confirmed, our problem is Cravens and others of his ilk. He doesn't know that the Tear of Blood has been dispersed. Dividing the diamond was genius and so very brave. But it does not solve our problem entirely. The armor is still a legendary relic. It contains pieces of the ancient tabernacle of God and remnants of spiritual history from all ages. And the sword of the Lord, as plain as it looks, is a thing from the mists, origins unknown—a magic charm to some who don't understand. In the wrong hands, the armor of God would be dissected and fought over. Claims, hot debates, backroom deals, tests and more tests . . . it would inevitably be enshrined in a museum or cathedral and prayed to!" She clicked her tongue. "Elijah, you are unusually logical about such situations. Do you have a suggestion?" Before I could think, she went on, "I had thought of burying it with my husband's remains back home."

I looked around. None of us liked the idea, but out of respect we considered it.

Mysteriously, Rob said, "Guys! 'Piece by piece they will rest in peace. Like the loved ones, in the ground.' Dowland's prophecy comes true!"

Dr. Eloise said, "My reasoning was this: I would select an aboveground crypt and use a casket—as if there were a body. The casket could hold the ashes and the armor. It is illegal to exhume a body without a court order, so our treasure would be safe—should we have need of it. The armor has served its purpose: to inspire you and the network, the fountainhead of this generation . . . perhaps the final generation." Wistfully she added, "I wish the whole network could see it somehow. Ah well, if memory of it grows dim, it can be circulated. But only a handful of us will know where it is."

"We never found the word on the sword," Reece said. "What about the legend that the sword speaks?"

She made a thin smile. "The Bible, which is the Word of God, speaks to us. That must be the answer."

I wasn't keen on the idea of burying the armor—not at all—but since we couldn't come up with a better idea, we agreed to go along with her decision—as long as we knew where the armor was.

We got called back to the first room. Dr. Eloise gasped as if she'd remembered something important and said in a rush, "Cremation is the Japanese custom, so do not be shocked. He is in Heaven and cares not a whit about his mortal body. He will put on a resurrection body as Jesus did when he came back from the grave. Are you prepar—"

Donovan whispered, "Brace yourselves."

The door in the wall opened and out came a huge tray carrying the skeleton of Dr. Dale—or most of it. Mei was the only one in our clan who wasn't a breath away from freaking out.

We stood there horrified as they picked up pieces of his bones with chopsticks and put them in a big urn. Mei quietly said to us, "I am sorry if this scares you. But I must be honest—we Japanese think American funerals are terrible. People touch a dead body! How awful!"

Rob had turned that nice shade of green again. I whispered harshly, "No *luftkrankheit*, Cuz, got that? No *luftkrankheit!*"

Dr. Eloise didn't flinch through the whole ceremony. I thought back over the two years I'd known her, how easily—even cheerfully—she coped with morbid stuff. Like Reece, she was stronger than she looked.

When Dr. Dale's remains were in the urn, Donovan shook our hands. "Thanks for being here with Eloise. It meant a lot to her. Each culture has its way of dealing with death, all pretty gruesome in one way or the other. I've seen my share. But it has to be done; people die. Sorry we didn't give you advance notice."

Rob murmured glumly, "It wouldn't have helped."

We met the rest of the people back at the mountain stream, but the spirit wasn't the same as before. Mei cried to think that Dr. Dale had baptized her a few days ago. We lay around on rocks like lazy walruses, listening to the stream, watching clouds float by, not saying much. Reece and I shared a rock, held hands, and stared at the sky.

In a daze she said, "Birds . . . cars . . . water . . . clouds . . . people . . . everything's rushing past us so fast, going away."

The next day the conference resumed at a quiet pace. There were Bible studies and discussions on science and archaeology—and "training." The training included group games to test how people worked together and handled stressful situations. We heard testimonies from around the world about miracles and brushes with death, updates about secret churches meeting in basements and forests and caves, stories about angel appearances, people rescued from torture, children "kidnapped" out of slavery. All of this stuff happening in The Window—and it was spreading.

I sat there on my floor pillow surrounded by my clan and people from every corner of the planet. *Where in the world have I been? Off in my safe little corner, oblivious.* Sure, I appreciated Mom and Dad protecting me from this kind of stuff when I was a grade-school kid—more grateful than ever. *But now*—I could hardly believe I was thinking it— *now I'm old enough and strong enough to do something about it. To be a part of it.*

We had dinner at the okeydokey-yaki place. Hester had gone with Dr. Eloise to rest, so Reece and I sat with Donovan, Li and Mei, and Baruti from Egypt. Baruti was a rugged, dignified man with gray hair, a wide face, and piercing eyes. As he poured batter on the grill, a chain around his neck swung forward with a medallion engraved with the tri-swirl design I'd seen on the tomb at Newgrange in Ireland.

"What's that?" I asked.

"The helix."

"What's it mean?"

He glanced at Donovan who gave him the go-ahead. "It's a universal symbol, claimed by Celts, Buddhists, Wicca, Hopi Indians, to name a few. But in truth it is older than them all and refers to tribal migrations, homecomings. It is the symbol of our network. You see, three times God commanded mankind to go into all the world. He gave Adam and Eve the whole earth to fill and subdue. Centuries later he told Noah's three sons the same thing." Baruti's voice boomed through the restaurant, "Go! Fill the earth!

"Instead, humankind gathered to build a tower with the hopes of installing a one-world government and reaching Heaven, making themselves gods." He fixed his eyes on Reece and me. "To spare mankind an early demise, the Lord confused the people's language and scattered them across the face of the earth."

Li said, "The third and final order came from God the Son: "'Go and make disciples of all nations.'"

Baruti fingered the medallion. "Correct. Three commands. Three people groups from the sons of Noah. Three types of warriors: riskers, wanderers, and those who stay."

Donovan pulled his medallion out from under his shirt and showed us. "Each is personalized, encoded with information: how many coils in each spiral, which direction they spin. Each element refers to a global position, a people group, and so forth. You probably didn't know this, but since you young people found the *Ogham* script on the shield, the Stallards suggested we add those markings to denote names and meeting places. Each medallion contains much more information than a military dog tag." He smiled. "And this symbol is a great conversation starter. People think it means everything from alien abductions to genetic mutation to prehistoric sun worship . . . which gives us an opportunity to talk about our mission: to fill the earth with God's truth and rescue his people."

"Most Christians wear crosses," Reece said skeptically.

Baruti stirred meat on the grill and said grimly, "Not all countries have the freedom you enjoy in the United States. In some places, if we wear crosses, we are sitting ducks."

Chapter 12

THE whole next day my clan withdrew. Marcus brooded. As far as I could tell, he was ticked that he'd been kept in the dark about his dad's secret career. Mei became Reece's shadow again, quiet and helpful, mostly because Reece still felt guilty about Dr. Dale's death. She was in a lot of pain because of the stress. Rob lost his comic edge and slept. I spent the afternoon at the stream. I'd gotten a glimpse of the big picture and needed time to take it in.

When Donovan and Hester left Nikko, Veronica kept Dr. Eloise company. Every morning I'd wake before sunrise and go for a run. Thoughts of the threatening flower nagged at me. The next few days of training with the members of the helix were something I'll never forget and can't really describe. These average-looking people knew everything about science and language and the Bible and spy-type stuff—all rolled into one. And there was this light in their eyes. . . .

At the final send-off, we gathered in a tight spiral so everyone was hugging everyone. As powerful prayers went up, the feeling of the Presence was so thick you could cut it with a knife. But for me personally, God was still silent.

On the final morning at Nikko, I got dressed at dawn and headed downstairs, planning to go to the stream to think and pray. I was getting my shoes on when Veronica appeared. She'd been waiting for me.

"Good morning, Elijah. Out for a run so early?"

"Yeah. I'm still on American time, I guess."

"Mind if I tag along?"

"Uh, not at all."

Answering my doubtful expression she pulled a form out of her pocket and said, "Don't worry, it's good news."

Late morning we checked out of the inn. The SOS came by to say good-bye, which was hard. It seemed we'd known them forever. Time had gone strange after losing Dr. Dale.

Apologizing for not going with us, Dr. Eloise sat a big suitcase down in front of me: the armor. "Where you are going next, you will not be welcome. I am speaking of the principalities and powers, not the people. This is a reminder of the power you have at your disposal. Know your enemy and, more importantly, know that in your weakness God is strong. Whatever happens, don't be afraid."

"What could happen?" I asked uneasily.

"Anything," she said with a sad smile. "Anything could happen. Pray the armor on. Follow the procedure that Dale set out for you. Enjoy your time with Mei. She can bring you on to Shimabara. I'll meet you at the castle there in a few days."

Rob chimed in knowingly, "Southern island. Eight hundred miles."

My clan got a taxi to the old station and tickets for the

train. Marcus had seen all this before in his travels, but we three Ohio *gaijins*—Rob, Reece, and myself—were impressed that kids, even grade-schoolers, could go all over a country by themselves on mass transit. The slow train took us back down through the dark mountains to the station where we picked up the bullet train again: a double-decker, even bigger and sleeker than the first.

"Honestly, Mei," I said as we boarded, "this is better than driving. You can sightsee, eat, sleep, go anywhere in luxury. Who needs a car?"

She grinned slyly. "Me."

For the next few hours, Rob and Mei chatted and ate *onigiri.* Marcus brooded. Reece slept against the window and didn't even flinch when other trains whooshed past just inches from her face. All the walking had been a drain on her, but she hadn't complained. She'd kept up.

We got off in Osaka and wound forever through the huge station. Without Mei, the Magdeline Five would have been lost lambs in a wild stampede of humanity. Snarfing down convenience-store meals, we caught a local for Kii Peninsula. For an hour we stood, packed like sardines, zipping through the humongous downtown again. I tried to imagine how all those people could live crammed together, so different from the wide-open spaces I called home. I felt small. Swallowed up.

As our train headed into the country, the crowd thinned out, and we found seats. Then it went dark. Not a darkness you see with your eyes; the August sun was blazing hot out there. I turned to Rob. "Did you feel that?"

"Feel what?"

"We just crossed over into . . . something. I don't know." Reece was writing postcards. I asked her, "Hey, Reece, did you feel something just happen, you know, spiritual?"

She sat still, as if listening. "Not really."

Marcus was asleep sitting up.

I moved over to Mei. "Remember the Stallards talking about that dream? Is there anything about a flower in your old religion?"

"I have been thinking about it, after Dr. Dale . . . There is the *Lotus Sutra,* a Buddhist scripture. In the temples many gods are standing or sitting on lotus flowers or holding lotus flowers. And we have prayer chants to the lotus."

Reece said, "But the dream said the flower had no fragrance or purpose. Lotus flowers are useful."

I said, "I don't think it's a real flower. It's symbolic."

At the station, Mei's aunt picked us up in a van. She told us in Japanese that she was very happy we'd come and hoped we enjoyed Japan. Mei said nothing about losing Dr. Dale. We all wanted to lay the horrible memory aside for a while, to relax and hang out on Mei's home turf. Marcus was pleased to have her all to himself again, no doubt about that.

Reece sniffed the air as we unpacked the van. "I smell peaches or apricots!"

"The valley is full of orchards, and it is harvest season," said Mei. "Our area is famous for fruit, especially *ume*, plums, which are made into wine and pickles. We will have fresh figs today—my favorite!"

The house was small and old-style Japanese-y, with paper screens and dark wood and a garden out the back. It was way cool. I warned Rob not to go ninja and demolish it.

Reece settled into Mei's room. Mei's two little cousins—Kenji and Taka, ages seven and ten—moved out of their room so we guys could have it. Mei had been teaching them a lot of English, but Marcus had to show off his Japanese. "Hey guys, *moukari makka?*"

They burst into guffaws and yelled, *"Bochibochi denna!"*

Mei acted like it was the coolest thing.

We sat around a square coffee table and had sandwiches and fruit. None of us *gaijins* had ever had fresh figs, and Rob snarfed up way more than his share. When her aunt went into the kitchen to get more, Mei whispered to us, "We will visit the mission house soon, but don't talk about it."

It was a short walk down a dirt lane to the Trentons' mission house. I guessed this was where the prayer journey would start. But I didn't know; this was still new to me. Marcus hung his arm around Mei the whole walk (which I don't mind saying bothered me; he wasn't doing right by Miranda). The Trentons had a nice American-looking place—two stories with a big yard. Mei introduced Paul, a short, friendly guy in his early forties, with light hair. His wife Lenora—small with dark hair and eyes—served tea in the living room. We did the small-talk stuff and then told about losing Dr. Dale. The Trentons had heard of him.

Reece explained that we'd come to visit Mei. "And we want to pray about the problems at your church."

He chuckled at us with that "they're just kids" look and said, "Mei mentioned that."

"We're here with the armor of God," I said seriously. "We need to know what to pray about. A soldier should know who the enemy is."

"Soldiers, huh?" Paul dropped down on the couch and smiled as if he were going to have to humor us.

"We mean it," Reece said toughly.

She's back, I thought with relief. *Unsinkable Reece is back.*

"Okay. If you want it, here it is," said Paul frankly. "Our numbers are few, our problems are many and severe: mental illness, cancers, abuses, suicide attempts, panic attacks, you name it. For years we've struggled. . . ."

"We'll pray for a whole day. Two days even," Reece said.

"Thank you," he said. Then after a long, curious pause, "I have to say . . . we get a lot of tourists from the States. They want to see the sights and sample the food. But we've never had any praying tourists." He smiled at us. "How 'bout you kids? Prayer warriors, huh? Okay, sure."

Remembering Dr. Dale's plan, I said, "We want to go to the temples and shrines around here and pray to God in places where he is ignored. But we won't be obnoxious."

"Is this a new kind of mission work?" Paul asked.

Marcus repeated what he'd heard at the conference, "It's very old. Like when Moses stood on the banks of the Red Sea with Pharaoh's army advancing. A bad fix! Millions of people between the enemy and the deep blue sea. That's when you pray like crazy and let God do his stuff."

"What's causing the problems?" Rob asked.

Paul entwined his fingers. "The problems are enmeshed, one tangled up in the other. They are offerings to idols—which are actually demons. There's praying to buddhas who are seen as men or gods, depending on whom you ask. There's nature worship: sun, mountains, trees. The nation's leaders were once considered descendants of the sun goddess. There's ancestor worship and the fear of displeasing the family, living and dead, if you don't perform certain rituals. Do you see how complicated it is?" he said sharply. "It's all intertwined! How does a citizen respect his culture and get untangled from its spiritual darkness?"

Reece said, "Mei did!"

Paul smiled. "But at great personal cost. Her family is not pleased. Her friends make fun of her."

Reece's face screwed up in a sad frown. "They do?"

Mei smiled. "It's okay. But we are taught to do what the family decides." Her eyes dropped. "I know that God is real; I know the Bible is true. But . . . my mother is right that it is scary to believe in one God. Many little gods to choose from are easier than one big, powerful God."

Marcus nodded, "He's untamable, all right. Unstoppable."

Mei went on. "I believe I can be a good Japanese and good daughter and a Christian too. I have a little more courage every day with the armor of God."

Paul studied his interwoven fingers defeatedly.

I asked, "How about we start tomorrow?"

"Sure," Paul said agreeably. "Mei wants to take you to the swimming hole, and today's a good hot day for it. The water is still swift from the typhoon," he warned, then chuckled, "which fortunately washed out the road to the local saloon. Their business has dropped off considerably!"

Rob said, "Hey, we flew in on that typhoon's tail!"

While the others made plans, I skimmed Paul's bookshelf.

"Looking for some reading material?" he asked.

"You have lots of religion books."

"It's my life's work."

"Do you have anything about the lotus?"

A short walk through a great-smelling plum orchard brought us to a clear stream bordered by marsh reeds.

The shady swimming hole was deep and calm, but in the narrow, shallow places, the current would sweep you right off your feet. It was as good as any water park! Needless to say, we guys did a lot of wrestling each other into the narrows. Several times Rob got washed downstream a hundred yards and dumped into a pool. (Funny how his

brave ninja cry and his "I'm pretending to drown" cry
were exactly the same!) Reece said we should use our new
names and pretend to be Japanese high school kids enjoying
break. We guys tossed Mei and Mayu around and made
them giggle. Shinobu, Ryo, and I—Takumi—forgot all our
troubles for a while. Fresh air and countryside—it suited me
fine.

After the swim Mei fixed barley tea and had us take a
rest. Kenji and Taka went with their mom to the market.
We stretched out on our pallets with the electric fan rotating
across us, the smell of fruit on the hot afternoon breeze. In
no time the guys were snoozing on either side of me. Out of
nowhere it hit me like a load of bricks: Dr. Dale was gone,
crushed right before my eyes. I suddenly felt sick. He'd left
me in the lead for spiritual warfare, and I didn't even know
what that meant yet. Dr. Eloise and the SOS were hundreds
of miles north. Sure Paul was an expert on religion, but since
we were just teenagers, he was skeptical of our mission.

Staring at the ceiling, I got to worrying about the lotus
again. On a whim I grabbed the Quella from my backpack
and punched in the word, expecting nothing. But it came
up: "Under the lotus plants he lies, hidden among the reeds
in the marsh. The lotuses conceal him in their shadow."

Conceal *who?* I sat up, scrolled up a few verses to see what
the passage was talking about. "Look at the behemoth. . . .
He ranks first among the works of God, yet his Maker can
approach him with his sword."

Behemoth? I looked it up: a powerful beast. *A beast hides under the lotus, concealed in its shadow? What beast?*

Mei's Aunt Sachiko fixed the best steak dinner we'd ever had, cooked with vegetables outside on a Korean-style grill. We stuffed ourselves then kicked back in the living room and played with Kenji and Taka, swapping English and Japanese words, tossing a ball around.

I took Reece for a bike ride so we could be alone for a while. We stopped at a bamboo forest and decided to explore it, squeezing through the dense stalks, not saying much. Reece commented, "Mei said this is the best place to be in an earthquake. The roots hold the ground together."

"That's good to know."

We went deeper into the grove until the road behind us disappeared. She stopped and looked at me. Her normally blue eyes had changed in the light of the forest to pale green.

"Elijah?"

"Uh-huh?"

"Do you think that lady's dream had anything to do with Dr. Dale?"

"I don't know."

I gave her a hug and half joked, "Hey, you're feeling okay, aren't you?"

"Yeah," she answered, a few seconds later adding, "There'll be a lot of walking tomorrow, I guess."

"Probably, but there's no hurry. We have all day. It's awesome in here, isn't it?"

"It's beautiful. Hey, what's your favorite drink so far?"

"Between the peach nectar and the royal milk tea," I said.

"Me too. I want to take some back on the plane for Mom and Darrell."

"Good idea."

A long time passed. The breeze swayed the lacy tops of the bamboo trees and gave us a feeling like we were at the top of Great Oak again. Only this time we weren't in the middle of a big fight when I kissed her and she kissed me back.

"Elijah," she asked quietly, "what do you think of the SOS, about what they do?"

"Sounds hard. But cool." I changed the subject. "You know, Dad should add a bamboo grove in Owl Woods." I didn't mention the long talk with Veronica—or the application form in my backpack.

Reece kept staring up at me until I took my eyes from the swaying treetops. Her expression was deep and unreadable. "About the SOS—you'd be good at it . . . Takumi."

I should have had a powwow that night to pray, but everyone was involved with the family: Marcus and Rob played hide-and-go-ninja through the neighborhood with the boys; Reece and Mei made a craft with Aunt Sachiko. I was out of it, thinking about the beast hiding under the lotus. Did that mean anything? I took a stroll through a plum orchard, watched the sun go down over one mountain and the moon rise above another. I wondered whether the danger was over—if Dr. Dale's death was the end of it. Part of me was relieved it had been him and not one of us. I felt like dirt thinking that, but I was up front with God and said I was sorry. I asked him to please break the silent treatment. *I'm not seeing your point. Are you silent because we don't have the real sword? Will you speak when we find it? What am I doing wrong?*

Wandering through the rows of plum trees in blue-green twilight, I noticed little shrines like the one I'd seen at the inn. They were everywhere: next to houses, along the road, in the lanes between the fields. Remembering the darkness I'd felt when we crossed into the peninsula, I had an inkling—more than an inkling, a knowing—that it was all around me now, even under me. *If there are gods in each of those shrines . . . but wait . . . they can't really be gods . . . because there's only one God . . . then . . . what are they? What is worshiped here? What has power? The lotus?*

Fighting the dread of going to the temples the next day, I pleaded, *God, where are you? Why did you take Dr. Dale and leave me on my own?* I wanted to back out but couldn't—I was the leader. I went back to Mei's house and tried to join in the fun everyone was having, looking at pictures and playing games . . . until Mei's uncle came home drunk and ordered everyone to bed so he could sleep in peace.

Mei was embarrassed. "I am sorry. It is like many business-men. They have work pressures, and they all drink together."

Kenji and Taka wanted to stay in the room with us *gaijins,* and Aunt Sachiko said it was okay. I figured they were afraid of their dad. I was beat, but having kids around reminded me of Camp Mudj—not that I was homesick.

In no time Marcus and Rob were out like lights; the boys horsed around in a wide beam of moonlight shining through the window, quiet because they didn't want to wake their dad. They looked like skinny little ghost monkeys playing, showing no signs of winding down. Figuring they'd be fine, I started to drift off myself, my eyes closed, my muscles relaxing. My mind was calm. Why was I worried about tomorrow anyway? The Nikko prayer walk had been awesome, everyone praising God together, Bible verses popping up like magic. Easy. Way cool . . .

Then I felt his breath in my ear and a growling, hissing whisper: "I told you to leave!"

A cold chill erupted along my spine and spread around my chest like long fingers, clamping around my heart. Not for a millisecond did I think it was Rob pulling a prank. I recognized the voice. With awful assurance I knew. *It's him. Again. Or another one like him.* I willed my eyes open. Hovering over me on his hands and knees like a dog—his eyes drilling into me with the same undiluted hate I'd seen before in a bookstore in Ireland—was Kenji. He glared at me ferociously, his head tipped, his lip curled.

My mind spun, my heart thudded. "No," I whispered firmly, "you . . . didn't." *You didn't tell me to leave, whoever you are, even if you're Kenji—which you're not. No one told me to leave.*

For a few more seconds, he hovered over me. I lay there washed in moonlight, his small black eyes pinning me down. Then he backed away, sat down, and glared at me sideways out of the corner of his eye. The expression went away—just dissolved—and he was Kenji again, a kid sitting there not wanting to go to bed early.

What do I do?!

Slowly, cautiously I reached over to him, afraid he'd bite me, wondering if he'd recoil. I put my hand on his back, like Dr. Eloise blessing the man who killed her husband. I prayed protection on both Kenji and me from whatever that thing was. Then I said, "Kenji, go to sleep now . . . Kenji."

He lay down and stared at the ceiling.

Over my short life, I'd had a lot of people mad at me: Dowland and his dog Salem, Theobald, the Mad River Boys, Miss Abner, the Brill brothers. And sometimes it was pretty scary. But all that was nothing to me now. It—whatever it was—hated that I existed, in this life or the next. That was clear as a bell.

All night I sat under the window and watched that patch of moonlight crawl across the room. Raw-nerved, exhausted, I stayed calm by thinking about home far away . . . teaching survival classes to grade-schoolers at Camp Mudj, horsing around with Nori and Stacy, building campfires for Dad, climbing Great Oak, wandering Council Cliffs, jogging down to Florence's for bacon and grits with the gang.

Chapter 13

IT was a clammy, misty morning. Mei's aunt woke the boys up early for their morning exercise class, so I got to sleep for a couple of hours. At breakfast Marcus sat with Mei and acted all smooth again. For some reason it irritated me—bad. I guess I was just tired, but with a tone that annoyed even myself I sneered, "Mei, you should have seen Skidmore and Varner at the masked ball last year. They were Lawrence of Arabia and Queen Nefertiri. A regular Hollywood couple, they were!"

Innocently Mei said, "Oh, I would love to see it! Rob, did you take pictures?"

Reece gave me a look.

Marcus eyed me and asked Mei, "Hey, Aizawa, how do you say *Get lost!* in Japanese?"

Mei said, *"Dokka ike!"* then changed the subject. "When I graduate, I want to study the travel in America so I can be in tourist business. Then I can work in the whole world if my grades are good and my parents will help me. I hope so!"

Mei and Rob went off talking about colleges and scholarships. Reece kept glancing at Marcus and me.

After breakfast when Reece and I were alone, she asked, "What's going on?"

"What do you mean?"

"I mean you and Marcus. It's like you're fighting over Mei."

"I don't want her to get hurt. He acts like he likes her."

"Maybe he does."

"What about Miranda?"

Reece huffed. "Mei can take care of herself. She's smart." She snipped, "You're not her mother."

Miffed, I stormed off to get ready for the prayer walk.

On our way to Paul's, I was thinking, *So who cares about Skidmore and Mei? Big stinking deal! And who cares what Reece thinks about what I think?*

Reece got in step beside me. "I'm sorry about earlier. Now tell me what's really wrong."

"We lost Dr. Dale; that's what's wrong." I couldn't tell her about Kenji. He was Mei's cousin, a seven-year-old kid. How could an entity be inside a kid? And anyway, we had a few more days at the house, so why freak everyone out when I could stand watch? Maybe I'd dreamed it. But I knew I hadn't. Maybe I'd gone loony.

"You're not the only one who's sad," she grumped.

"I know! What's that got to do with anything?"

"You're being all distant and moody," she huffed.

Rob said, "Yeah, Takumi, and don't keep telling me not to 'go ninja' every place. You keep forgetting that I'm older and make better grades . . . so *dokka ike!*"

"You *dokka ike!* Fine, make a fool of yourself in another country. You're a *henna gaijin* anyway!"

Marcus scowled at me and muttered, "Creep."

By the time we got to the Trenton house, no one was speaking to me.

Paul loaded us into his van and gave us wary looks; you could cut the tension with a knife. I rode shotgun so I wouldn't have to talk to the others. Paul said, "Elijah, you were asking about the lotus. I did a little research last night. The use of the lotus in worship goes back thousands of years to ancient Egypt. And in Greek mythology, eating the lotus lulls a person into a state of dreamy forgetfulness." He paused uneasily and handed me papers. "I'd never read the Buddhist teachings of the lotus before last night. You might want to look over those excerpts of the *Lotus Sutra*."

I skimmed a few pages and didn't know whether to laugh or be completely creeped out.

Getting us back on track, Reece said, "Hey, let's sing first like we did at Nikko."

Winding through narrow village streets, the Magdeline Five tried to make the best of it, singing and waving at fruit farmers while Paul greeted them in Japanese. We turned up a steep, narrow street to a temple on the hill and parked beside it. Facing out over the city, the brand-new temple of natural wood had big pillars, a curved roof, and fancy gold trim. The landscaping was awesome, with sculpted trees and stone paths and fishponds. Up the terraced hill behind the temple was a cemetery. The place seemed deserted. Paul got out, uncertain as to what to do.

I said, "We split up. Everybody take your Bible. Don't make a scene or talk loud. We respect their property. And everyone stay where I can see you."

Paul chuckled at me in a fatherly way. "It's safe here."

Reece said to Paul, "Everyone wanders and stays open to what God wants him to pray. That's how we've seen it done. I'll stay here by the entrance, okay?"

"I'll go on up through the cemetery," said Rob.

"Far side," said Marcus and took off.

Mei said, "I will walk through the garden."

"What god is worshiped here?" I asked Paul as we wandered around the front of the temple.

He smiled. "Good question. Oriental cultures are known for their many gods." He picked up a rock and sat it on a bench. "If I bow to that, it becomes *kami*, a god. A god can be anything. There are millions."

"Millions?"

Along the edge of the curved roof of the temple were round tiles with a flower design on each one. "There's your lotus," he said, "an object of importance, though I'm not sure why. In some sects the *Lotus Sutra* itself is worshiped. And the symbol of the lotus supposedly has great power."

"Why would people worship a book?"

"As a ritual to get to nirvana—which we Westerners think means Heaven."

"But really means extinction," I recalled Rob's research.

"You'll read in that excerpt that dragons and other

nonhuman creatures supposedly protect the religion. Ten demon daughters and the Mother of Devil Children pronounce curses on anyone who fails to heed their spells or tries to disrupt the teaching of the lotus."

I read aloud, "'Their heads will split into seven pieces like the branches of the arjaka tree.'" I skimmed more pages and added dryly, "Nice. So these curses are against us? It says that anyone who tries to stop the spread of buddha worship will go into Hell and be reborn as a scabby dog and plagued with starvation, or as a donkey to be whipped and beaten, or as a serpent to be devoured by insects, or as a blind, deaf, dimwitted, hunchbacked human. There are pages of curses."

Paul smiled grimly. "All this in allegiance to the Thus Come One, most honored of two-legged beings." He quoted, "'I am the World-Honored One! None can rival me!'"

"Is this for real?"

"To those who believe it, yes."

"Who is the Thus Come One, World-Honored One?"

He just shook his head. "Supposedly a buddha. But we know from the Bible that Satan is the honored prince of this world, even though he leads it astray."

"This was Mei's religion?" I asked in disbelief. "Extinction and curses by demons?"

"She probably never read the *Lotus Sutra* or understood the rituals. Religion is more like tradition here, for good luck."

There were no gates at the temple, so I circled the whole place, praising God for his power and for using me and my friends for some great purpose, even if I couldn't see it yet. Even if I didn't feel it. Even if I didn't like them very much right now. It was lonely up on that hillside—just us five, a bunch of dead people, and Paul, one of the few believers in the whole city. I missed the big youth group at home. I missed Dr. Dale's calm presence, and wondered if he'd been taken out because he was our leader.

I wondered if I was next.

Mei was reading her Bible in the garden. I sat down with her. "Did you ever read any lotus sermons or worship them? Did your aunt . . . or cousins?"

She thought. "I don't know . . . but one of the favorite goddesses in Japan—*kannon*—has a lotus prayer for good luck. We say that prayer."

I left Mei in the garden so I could find a place to be alone and think. *Lotuses in stone and bronze. Flowers with no fragrance or purpose. Threats from dreams: don't move me or try to change me! Lying threats: I told you to leave! Demon eyes glaring out of the head of a nice little kid.* Shaken, I looked up the familiar armor passage and read it thirstily: "Our struggle is not against flesh and blood, but . . . against the powers of this dark world and against the spiritual forces of evil in the heavenly realms. Therefore put on the full armor of God. . . ." I put on, prayed on, every piece and wondered stupidly why I hadn't done it sooner. Wondered why I hadn't prayed it on the Magdeline Five.

Paul drove us to a second temple on another hill. We passed a children's graveyard with a guardian god standing on a lotus. "This is one of many pilgrimage places. Last night while doing research, I realized for the first time that this whole peninsula is dedicated to religions involving the lotus." He looked at me curiously. "What made you ask?"

I told him about the lady's dream and about feeling a huge darkness as we entered the peninsula. He listened but had no comment.

Mei and Reece found a spot in the shade and read Scripture to each other. Paul joined Marcus and Rob as they walked a path lined with idols. I wandered the parking lot, pacing below the huge temple, trying to think about God, trying to call on his power. But I didn't feel any power. My heart wasn't in it. All I could say was, *God, you are God. I know that. There is only you. The other gods are no gods. There is only you.* Finally I dropped down on the curb, tired and sweaty, punched in the lotus Scripture on my Quella, and dwelled on it a long time. This prayer journey was nothing like Nikko's. It was lame, and we were glum and hot and tired.

By the third day without sleep, I was running on fumes. I couldn't sleep for imagining what that thing—Lotus— might do to me in my sleep. It was Sunday. Kenji and Taka were still asleep when my clan grabbed breakfast and walked down to the Trenton house for church, their red diamond jewelry glinting like fire in the morning sun.

The downstairs of Paul's house was fixed up with metal chairs and a pulpit. A dozen people came; the only girl our age had an odd look about her. As she sat down by us, Mei whispered that she had a mental problem. The service was simple, but everything was in Japanese. We four Americans were pathetic singers; we didn't know the words or tunes.

Paul introduced us and asked us to say a few words about ourselves; he would translate. Reece took center stage first, saying how we'd come from America to visit Mei and to pray for their church. She was her usual upbeat self; they loved her. My spiel was brief. It was hard to concentrate, fighting off sleep like I was. The people were appreciative and nice, but honestly, I was glad when church was over.

They set up tables in the front yard, brought food out, and we had a picnic. One older lady had handmade purses for the girls. We guys got kites with samurai warrior designs on them. By mid-afternoon the church people had gone home. We went back to Mei's. My head felt like it weighed a ton; I wanted to find a spot under a tree and sleep, but Mei wanted to take us to the coast for dinner. *Okay, Creek,* I told myself, *be excited or you'll look like a jerk.*

A half-hour drive got us to the Pacific Ocean. The overlook was so much like the Cliffs of Morte, it was spooky; everyone said so. We got quiet, gazing out over the thrashing sea with the late afternoon sun behind us, a sheer drop-off yards ahead. This was the suicide cliff Mei had told us about at Cathedral Cave, the beautiful place to die.

Reece said, "Okay, we all stay waaaay back."

"Got it!" Rob agreed.

"Where are the fences and warning signs!?" Marcus griped.

There was no rail and only one sign in Japanese with a cross on it. Mei translated. "It says 'The Phone Call of Life. Before making a final decision, please talk with us! We are waiting for your call.'" She read the verse at the bottom: "Jesus said, 'I am the light of the world. Whoever follows me will never walk in darkness, but will have the light of life.'" Mei paused seriously. "I have been here many times, but I didn't understand this verse. I was blind to it, but now I see." Unexpectedly she threw her arms around me, then around each of the others. Considering that Japanese don't touch much in public, it was a shock. She cried, "Thank you again for saving my life at Cathedral Cave. I would have missed my whole life with my friends!"

"It's okay," I said, "we're the Magdeline Five. Nothing will ever change that."

I told you to leave!

Yeah, right. It was a big fat lie to scare me off. And it almost worked. I wished Dr. Dale was here. I wanted to call Dom Skidmore. What time was it in the States, 5:00 in the morning? Nope, I had to handle this myself. *God, talk to me. I need an English translation of what's going on.*

I kicked back through dinner while the others chatted

and wondered what was wrong with me, why I was so quiet. When the rest went to sleep, I propped myself against the bedroom wall. Mei's uncle had come home drunk again, so if I had tried to make Kenji and Taka sleep in the living room, I'd have looked like a totally mean *gaijin*. And I'd have worried about Reece and Mei all night. Kenji had acted like a normal raucous kid except for that one moment, but I didn't trust him. It was my job to protect my clan. I started thinking about how to get Mei out of here once we left the country.

By 2:00 in the morning, my eyelids were lead weights; my eyes sandpaper. Throwing on shorts and a T-shirt, I took the armor in the suitcase out to the front porch. I unpacked it in moonlight, keeping an ear toward the open front door. Handling each piece, I imagined my clan back around a campfire at Silver Lake where we'd first analyzed it—things had been simpler then. I put on the right arm of fellowship, made a fist of the ragged glove. *We need to go back to the beginning, get* koinonia *again. We still have a day of spiritual warfare at the town's main* torii *gates and at those little farm shrines. For whatever good it will do. Really . . . what's the point of praying and reading? Nothing happens. Yeah, yeah, I know faith is being "certain of what we do not see," but how are we supposed to believe what we can't see? Oh . . . oh great! Now I'm losing my faith—with the shield of faith lying here right in front of me. That's just terrific. Peachy as peach nectar!* I lay the arm down and sat gazing at the full moon. I silently called up to Heaven, *Why won't you talk to me? This prayer journey's almost over and getting lamer by the minute. Where are the magic Scriptures and the happy floaty feelings?*

No answer. I wanted to run, blow off some steam, but couldn't. I had to stand watch over the house in case that thing came back. An ageless, evil thing I didn't understand, didn't know how to deal with. At home I could have climbed Great Oak to clear my head, but here I was stuck. Trapped. Suddenly I just stood up and screamed inside, *Hold on a minute! Satan may be prince of the world, but you're the big king of the universe, so you baby-sit for a while!"* Angrily I took off. Down the lane past darkened houses and creepy little shrines I ran barefoot, pretending I was in Owl Woods and knew every dip and curve in the path. My curses raged at God for leaving me high and dry. *Yeah, I'm cursing. So I'm bad now! Just lost the breastplate of righteousness, I guess. I'm soooo bad!*

The moon cast my own swift shadow ahead of me. I wanted to run over it, stomp it. Stomp myself. Shadowy arms and legs pumped; my fugitive self was flat and formless slithering ahead of me. No matter how hard I ran, I'd never stomp it.

I zigzagged blindly through the neighborhood, past orchards and rice fields. The swimming hole came into view—black as ink under the tree-lined bank, dark as Gilead on a moonless night. I didn't pause to think. I ran full force and dove in. Baptism into nothingness. Nirvana. Extinction. Swallowed up by the cold inky water, I forced myself to stay under until my lungs burned. *No peace, no faith, no truth, no nothing! I didn't want to hear from you anyway. Keep your words and your wordless sword! It's just a hunk of metal anyway. Probably not even the real thing. No word on it . . . no word from YOU!*

When my air-starved lungs couldn't take it anymore, I jettisoned myself to the surface and hungrily gasped air. I threw myself back and floated in the swimming hole like a dead man, eyes open, seeing nothing. Nothing but leaves, low and black and lacy with the moon a silver disc beyond. I'd seen moon shadows a million times, seen stars in a charcoal sky above Great Oak, but this time it was different. Everything was alive, watching me.

Slowly the current began to move me across the swimming hole and toward the narrows. I drifted. The current picked up, faster, faster, shooting me across the narrows . . . and into a tangle of reeds. I found myself caught in a kind of whirlpool. I tried to paddle but got nowhere, the reeds thick and slimy hindering me. *Hidden in the reeds of the marsh, under the lotus he lies. The beast.* Suddenly frantic, corkscrewing to free myself, I paddled like crazy but got nowhere. *I'm going down!* My feet couldn't find bottom to push off, only slimy tangles—below, above, all around. Fingers of terror tightened around my ribs again. *I want up. Up! Get me back in the current, in the current. Don't let me drown! I'm close to the current, but which way? I need you! Which way is out? I need you!*

Then I looked up. I caught sight of the watery moon and got my bearings, all the while thrashing wildly until the current grabbed me like a cool, strong hand. I was shot through the narrows like an arrow, dumped downstream into the next quiet pool.

I squished all the way back through the sleeping neighborhood, the moon casting my shadow behind me now. I plopped down on Mei's porch, my mind strangely quiet. I repacked the armor. *Talk to me, sword.*

"Elijah?" came a voice behind me. I jumped. Mei came out on the porch. "Are you okay? How did you get wet?" she laughed. "Did you fall into the *ofuro?*"

"Can't sleep," I said wearily. "I went for a swim. Jet lag, I guess." Which was a lie. I lied with the belt of truth at my feet. I was slipping backwards on every count. *I need help.*

She sat beside me. "I finished my papers for school, and then I was thinking of the word on the sword. There was no piece of the sword from the helmet."

"Right."

"May I look again?"

"Sure. The armor's yours too."

I followed her inside with the suitcase. We sat on the floor near an end-table lamp. She examined the helmet, her delicate fingers running over every edge. "I think it must be inside, like the other pieces."

"We all looked. Rob even used a magnifying glass."

Her patient examination of the helmet brought a calm over me. I started to breathe again. "Hey, um, it's none of my business, but you and Marcus . . ."

She got shy. "He is so kind to me."

"Uh-huh."

"He is helping me with a problem. I . . . I like a boy at my school, but he makes fun of me for worshiping the American god. Marcus has a problem with Miranda who has no belief too. Marcus talks to me about it and makes me feel better." She giggled. "He promises—but it is a joke—he promises that he will not get married until I do. And if I can't find someone, then he will marry me. He's great."

"Yeah," I said guiltily, "he's pretty cool."

Mei said, "You and Reece—uh, Mayu . . . you are very lucky. You have the same beliefs."

I grinned. "Yeah."

Her fingertip stopped on one of the lines etched into the helmet. "This cut is deeper. I think there is a separate piece." She dashed to the kitchen on tiptoe (while I sat there feeling like a big clod of dirt about Marcus) and came back with a paring knife. She slipped the point into the crack, working it ever so gently until it lifted a fraction of an inch. "Ah! I think this is like our secret boxes. You must move it just the right way to get it open." Patiently she worked, moving and sensing, a hair to the right, then left, cleaning bits of mud that we'd missed after fishing it out of Silver Lake.

The piece rose by degrees and finally lifted off. Inside was a secret compartment barely an eighth of an inch thick and lined with wool. Pressed into the cloth was a layer of glitter. She lifted it out. "It is like chain mail only—aaahh!" She dropped it into the compartment and looked at her open hand. Her fingertips were covered with blood.

"What in the world?" I said.

Mei got a hankie from her pocket and blotted her fingers.

I reached in to pick up the mesh.

She cried, "It hurts you!"

I picked up the very edge with my fingernails. It was mesh, a long, ragged scrap of woven metal made of what you might call flat metal threads—fine and sparkling and razor sharp.

"Should we wake the others?" she asked excitedly.

I suddenly remembered Kenji, how I'd left the others in God's hands while I stupidly half tried to drown myself. "I'll go check on 'em." I looked in on the guys and the cousins, then Reece. I went back out to the living room where Mei had spread the piece over the arm of the couch. I said, "They're sound asleep. Maybe the words are engraved here like they were on the chain mail."

We had no magnifying glass. Carefully, I picked it up and held it under the light. Mei and I were excited. I was sure we'd found the word.

That next morning we showed the others the shiny ragged mesh and brainstormed over it. The others were as excited as Mei and me, but no word could be found. We needed Dr. Eloise's linen tester.

We did the last maneuvers of the prayer journey in better

spirits, strolling the lanes between farms, smelling the fruit drying, watching misty clouds drift up the mountainside. *Fresh air close to the Pacific coast, homegrown food, a swimming hole—a perfect place to live.* Except for little shrines to gods of agriculture and who-knows-what-else lurking throughout the village and orchards. At every little *torii,* Reece would say her verses from the *Warrior.* Honestly, it was a little embarrassing to sing songs about Jesus by ourselves in a plum grove. But we did. We followed an overgrown set of stone steps up a hillside and found a newly planted shrine in the bushes. They were cropping up everywhere.

Paul took us downtown to the largest shrine in town with a gate as big as the one in Nikko. We paused while Reece did her thing. This time I said it with her. The shrine was a large, open area ringed with awesome red and gold buildings of different sizes, fishponds, and arched bridges. I circled the space and opened my heart up to God. Then I put on the spiritual armor I'd thrown off the night before.

Paul chatted in Japanese with the Shinto priest. I stood beside him, taking in the rhythm and complexity of the language. Having suffered through Latin, I was impressed at how Paul had mastered another language.

We left after Reece had put her hand on the giant pillar one last time and said tiredly, but with determination, "'This is the gate of the LORD.'"

Chapter 14

SHIMABARA—on Kyushu island. I've never had such trouble getting to a place in my life! After good-byes at the station (I gave Kenji a bear hug while praying in earnest, *God, whatever you do in this demon situation, do it, okay?*), we waited for the train. Rob complained about the driving rain.

Marcus said, "Count your blessings, Shinobu. We're under a roof. You Americans are spoiled. In some places in the world, just walking across the street could get you shot."

"No more arguing please," Mei said firmly.

Suddenly cheerful, Rob said, "Mei and I have figured out the cheapest way to get there: overnight bus. We head back toward Osaka, get a taxi at the fifth stop before Sakai, and catch the bus there."

I didn't care as long as I got some sleep.

Only that didn't happen.

The local train was packed. We got off at the right stop for a taxi stand, but there wasn't one. The street was deserted, with one convenience store open. Mei asked for directions at the counter and turned to us, flustered. "The closest taxi stand is in that direction." She pointed down a dark street. "Not far."

"Let's hope so," I said. We set out into the warm, sloppy night.

We took turns carrying Reece and her luggage for the next twenty minutes. Wheezing, Rob cried, "Not far? Hogwash! Don't people here know what *not far* means? Does *not far* mean *not near* in Japanese, 'cause that's what I'm getting!"

"The Japanese walk more and talk less," Marcus said with threat in his voice. "That's why they live longer."

Ignoring him, Rob said, "I see streetlights over there."

"The store clerk said this way," Mei argued.

I whispered to Reece, "Pray, Mayu, pray!"

We stopped in a pedestrian tunnel under a highway to get out of the weather and take a breather. I offered to scout ahead, but the others were afraid we'd get separated. Out of nowhere a businesswoman appeared in a suit and high heels. She stopped dead at the sight of us *gaijins* lurking in the dark tunnel. Mei stepped out, apologized, and asked directions. A couple of lefts and rights and we were on the main street. Rob frowned at his watch. "We have fifteen minutes to get to the bus terminal. Start flagging taxis!"

"Here comes one!" Reece stepped toward the curb.

I barked at her to get back. "Let Mei and Shinobu do that. Ryo, you guard the luggage."

"I can flag!" he barked back.

"You're too scary."

Mei got us a cab and ordered the driver to hurry. He barreled through traffic, pulled down a side street, and screeched to a halt at a lonely open-air bus stand thick with spiderwebs and big gnarly spiders.

"Where's the station?" Rob whined.

Mei handed bills to the driver. "No station. We get out."

The cabbie unloaded our luggage, pulled out, and once again we were by ourselves on a dark road at night. The time came and went for the bus to come.

Rob eyed his watch. "I bet it was early, and we missed it."

The overnight bus barreled in ten minutes late; we cheered in relief and sloshed up the steps. It was nice and super clean with a TV up front. Down a few steps were a restroom and a tiny tea station half the size of a shower stall. We got free blankets, bitsy pillows, and paper slippers, and then we took turns opening our backpacks in the aisle to get dry clothes and change in the little restroom. The others on the bus—mostly businessmen—politely ignored us.

Our chairs only reclined so far, with no way to turn over or lie flat. It was a long, achy night, but at least we were dry and going somewhere. After Gilead, I'd vowed never to complain about accommodations again.

At daybreak, Rob woke us up and fixed tea at the little tea station, mostly so he could make the same lame joke over and over: "If anyone needs me, I'll be *downstairs in the kitchen.*" (And I have to say here that Japanese people can get more stuff into a tiny space and make it work than I've ever seen.)

The overnight bus dumped us out at a sweet station in Nagasaki with an ocean view and tons of vending machines.

We were on Kyushu island! Marcus and I ran around the parking lot to get the kinks out. We all grabbed a Japanese breakfast, brushed our grungy teeth, and washed our faces.

"To the next train!" said Rob, waving his map, his face dripping and shiny.

Easier said than done. The stop where we could catch a bus for the next station was half a mile. I could tell that Reece was beyond worn out. But it was a clear, sunny day; we were dry and full of tea and *onigiri;* the rain and the overnight bus ride had beaten all the complaining out of us.

The local to Shimabara was slow and old, *clackety-clack*ing along. We didn't care; our car was half empty with plenty of space to stand, sit, or stretch out. We didn't know why the Stallards had wanted to end our trip here—and didn't care. The darkness had faded, and we were on our way to a shogun castle with hours of nothing to do but hang out. Rob snapped pictures of rice fields. I made myself swear if he went into ninja mode in the castle, I'd keep my trap shut. Marcus was in another world. Mei wrote in her journal. Reece curled up on the seat next to her, using her backpack as a pillow. I watched her sleep and thought about a million things: *How far was it to Samoa? How many days by boat? If I worked it so the others could go, who'd pay for their tickets? The SOS kids were great, but we were the Magdeline Five. Would we need different clothes? Biggest question of all, what would our parents say?* I read over the application form stashed in my backpack and thought of Mom and Dad and the twins and

THE CARPET OF BONES

Camp Mudj. I wondered what it meant to be a Magdelinian, what it might mean to be the third Elijah, and why I'd been targeted by Lotus. Questions were as thick and tangled as those spiderwebs four hundred miles ago.

As the town came into view, Mei chirped to Marcus, "We need a travel talk, Ryo, like you made in Ireland!"

Straightening an invisible tie, Marcus came back to planet Earth and said with flair, "As the traveler approaches the quaint village, he will pass verdant countryside panoramas. Brilliant rice fields in August make a veritable patchwork quilt. If one is alert, one may catch a glimpse of sun-washed sea. And looming ahead, the jagged peaks of—what's that mountain, Mei?"

Rob answered, "It's Mt. Unzen, a volcano; and there's a hot springs spa there."

"Ah, the famous Mt. Unzen," Marcus droned on. "Road-weary wanderers flock to its healing waters and breathtaking view. Daring mountain climbers hazard its steep slopes. At the foot of the mountain rests Shimabara, a quaint village—"

"You already said 'quaint village,'" Rob jabbed.

Marcus ignored him, his eyes locking on something ahead. "Whoa . . . get a load of that!"

Hogging the whole center of town, a huge, white Japanese castle rose up above modern houses and businesses, strangely out of place in this century.

We hauled ourselves and our luggage off the train and

up a short hill through the outer wall of Shimabara Castle. Acres of low gardens and pools where the moat used to be surrounded the stone foundation wall. And waiting for us on a bench and admiring the lily pads was Dr. Eloise. "Hello, children. Who's ready for some exciting history?"

The castle was way cool, a big square hallway on each floor with displays of samurai weapons and armor, paintings of battles and burning castles—lots of war stuff. Rob kept a pretty good lid on his primal screams and air-chopping.

Faking disappointment, Marcus said to him, "Sorry, Shinobu, but it's just not the same without the skirt."

"This town was the last stand of Christianity in Japan in the old days," explained Dr. Eloise. "Dr. Dale wanted very much for you to see it." She smiled a faraway smile. "The year was 1637. Faith in one God was spreading through the country when the leaders, for many reasons—some political, some purely evil—saw belief in Jesus as a threat. To make matters worse in this region, there was a very high tax oppressing the farmers, the government taking up to eighty percent of their crops. Those who didn't comply with the tax law or the religious prohibitions could anticipate torture or death. Believers were beheaded, crucified," she pointed out the window toward Mt. Unzen, "or thrown into the volcanic crater. Children were killed beside their parents. Each torture was devised to be more horrible than the one before. Many thousands died. It was in the thick of this persecution that a boy of sixteen named Amakusa Shiro, a young believer who sympathized with the farmers, led a rebellion against the fierce shogunate.

"For months the rebels held off the more powerful army, but eventually they ran out of food and ammunition. Thirty-seven thousand died in one battle. This castle museum gives us the story; we'll take a shuttle to the actual site. And we must see the statue." She smiled at me mysteriously.

"This is *fumie*," Mei said, pointing into a display case at a small square piece of wood engraved with something. "It is a picture of Jesus. The leaders made Christians step on Jesus' face. If they did not, they were killed." She turned to us. "This is why it is still hard to be a Christian here."

Rob's eyes got wide. "You mean we could be killed?"

She laughed. "It is safe now, silly. We are civilized country. But our culture says it is better to do the same as everyone else. We have a saying, 'The nail that sticks up will be hammered down.' Being the same is very important to us. We will gladly give up personal wishes to be part of the group. To be a Christian is to be different."

Rob said, "Sorry, Mei, I couldn't do that: be the same."

Marcus snorted, "You got that."

Dr. Eloise said, "Our cultures are different for good reasons, Rob. America is a young country; the Europeans who settled America were adventurers—risk-takers with individualism and grit. The Japanese, on the other hand, have lived on a small island for many centuries. Yet they have found a way to maintain peace in close community."

"Makes sense," Marcus said. "My people have their own ways too." He did a jiggy dance. Rob chopped his neck. The girls rolled their eyes. I laughed and then got a pang in my gut. *The Mag Five. My clan, together . . . for how much longer?*

There were other buildings to see, but Dr. Eloise steered us through the gardens to a bronze statue of a young warrior wearing old-style Japanese clothes, a cross, and a sword. His hands were folded, his face lifted to Heaven. "This is Amakusa Shiro," she said, "the boy who led the rebellion in hopes of stopping the persecution. He risked everything for his convictions. Can you imagine that kind of courage?"

I glanced at Mei, wondering what she thought of him, a kid like herself killed by his own people.

But Reece was looking at me.

We caught a shuttle to the Hara fortress ruins where the final stand actually took place. It was an overgrown hill ringed with remnants of stone walls. In spots the ground was raked clean and measured off for excavation.

"Why are we here?" Rob asked.

Dr. Eloise said, "Children, remember the metal cross at the center of the shield of faith? Dale's research has led us to conclude that it came from here. There at those bare spots where the fortress once stood, scientists unearthed a carpet of bones dating back to the rebellion. In the final days of the siege, the rebels were unable to hold off their enemy any longer. All hope of victory vanished, and thousands chose to burn rather than surrender. But in the fortress ruins along with the bones, several crosses were found, apparently cast from the last of the bullets. Some of those crosses were even found under skulls, suggesting that believers placed their precious crosses in their mouths so they would be the last things to burn."

Silently we looked across the quiet field, its tall grass blowing in the breeze under a sunny blue sky. Hard to believe it had been a battleground.

Rob said, "Someone who knew about the armor of God was here on that day?"

"Someone survived?" Reece asked.

Dr. Eloise said, "He would have taken his cross, gone underground, and become one of the 'hidden Christians,' those who worshiped in secret for generations under threat of death." Her voice hardened. "Souls as indestructible as those little crosses. Children, you must grasp this: in spite of the carpet of bones, they all made it through the fire! As will the millions who stand their ground to the end. We must remember—not that they died, but that they live!"

Dr. Eloise pulled a small plastic bag from her purse. She raised it high and whispered, "'Can these bones live?'" and poured out a handful of ashes. The ocean breeze carried the little cloud across the grassy field. She dusted off her hands and smiled. "They will live, when the number is complete, when the bones of martyrs carpet the earth."

Chapter 15

✕✕

"I need to rest," said Reece on the shuttle back to town. Her face was strained and red from all the stair climbing.

"The youth hostel is four blocks from the castle," Mei said. "Should we rest before checking in?"

Reece took a ragged breath. "I can make four blocks."

We made it to the hostel, but the door was locked. A sign in Japanese hung over the door. Mei worried over Reece. "Oh, Mayu! They are closed and will not open until 6:00!"

Reece strained to say, "That's okay. Let's go to a restaurant, get something to drink . . . sit down."

Rob studied the map. "Hey, the waterfront is that way. There's a park. It'll have benches."

Mei said cheerily, "I will bring food and drinks. A picnic!"

"How far?" I asked.

"Two more blocks," Rob answered.

"Two blocks," Reece grimaced. "I can do two blocks."

I stooped. "Hop on. Piggyback."

The park was a huge waterfront lawn with a playground on the far side. Fishing and tour boats lined the pier. Not a soul was around. I spotted a short tree with a trunk that looked like a bunch of vines twisted together. I slapped my hands together and went into Camp Mudj mode. "Okay, kids, nap time! On your bunks!"

"What bunks?" Marcus said flatly.

I ran to the grassy spot under the tree, tossed down my backpack, pulled out my jacket, spread it on the ground, and started blowing up my flight pillow. "My bunk's ready. Anybody need help with theirs?"

They bought the idea.

"Perfect," Reece said with relief. "Let's rest then eat."

We settled ourselves under the thick viney tree, which Dr. Eloise identified as *ficus superba*. Rob named it the Elf Tree. We were exhausted from the complicated trip and dazed by Dr. Eloise's story of Amakusa Shiro and the carpet of bones. We were tired of bickering and relieved the prayer journey was over. I was fried from night watches for Lotus. The cool afternoon breeze felt great. Magdeline, Ohio, was a galaxy away. Soon we were all flat on our backs staring up at the Elf Tree. Mei felt funny being there. Only homeless people sleep in the park, she said. We told her it was okay to do weird things; she was with *henna gaijins*.

Rob said quietly, "Right now we *are* homeless."

"Not bad, eh?" I observed.

"Not bad until the next typhoon," he said darkly.

"Aw, it's just water," I said flippantly.

We lay there snickering about old times—me getting dunked with the ice chest on Devil's Cranium, our last powwow with Mei. Dr. Eloise was snoring already.

"Open air—no boundaries. This is my turf," I murmured.

Lured by the sounds of seagulls and light traffic, a warm

breeze, a magic tree . . . in minutes we all were asleep.

An hour later I woke, every muscle in my body at perfect rest. I looked around. The others were out like lights. Here we were: homeless teens asleep under an elf tree with an old archaeologist in an empty park in a foreign country, with the armor of God wadded up in a suitcase. *Traveling freak show.* I chuckled to myself for a long while at how ridiculous it all was. I was dead tired but wide awake, relaxed but braced for another surprise attack from Lotus. *How'd I ever get here?*

My thoughts drifted to Amakusa Shiro's statue, how he wore a cross and a sword, with his eyes on Heaven and a smile on his face. I wondered if he really was glad to die young, or if that was just the sculptor's idea. He and thirty-seven thousand snuffed out, his dreams up in smoke, his rebellion crushed. *Bummer.* Here I thought this trip was going to be a fun visit with Mei and a chance to see Japan. Instead, I'd been chewed up and spit out; set up, singled out, chosen by God? For what—to eventually be bronzed and stuck beside a castle with a pretend smile on my face for future generations to stare at? I sat up, miffed. *Were those prayer journeys meant to make me strong for some future trial? Well, they didn't. Nothing happened. Three years searching for your armor. A trip around the world. Why? To see Dr. Dale die? To be sneered at by this Lotus thing from the ancient past? You've shot me into the air like an arrow, and I don't know where to land. Don't I get a say?* I begged. *I need a word from you, El-Telan-Yah! I am thirsty to hear from you!*

I got up and quietly staggered to the water's edge. Cruise boats bobbed, the smell of saltwater filled the air. I was back in Low Country, where we'd gone shrimping and had fought unseen enemies in the dark. Everything seemed to be coming full circle. I looked back at my clan, like fairy-tale characters under a magic spell. *I gotta make a decision about the SOS. I gotta get Mei out of that house. I gotta talk to Dad. And Reece.* My mind a wreck, I got the Quella out of my pants pocket and punched ON. Nothing. *Battery's dead.* I laughed darkly. *Figures.* I went back to the tree where Reece's study Bible lay beside her. I picked it up, stuck my finger in a page and threw myself onto my jacket faceup, with an umbrella of leafy green above me. *Whatever you have to say, I'll listen*, I said grudgingly.

My finger had stuck in Isaiah chapter 28. Oh great. Old Testament, the dull stuff: "Woe to that wreath, the pride of Ephraim's drunkards, to the fading flower, his glorious beauty, set on the head of a fertile valley—to that city, the pride of those laid low by wine!"

I stopped. *Fading flower? Glorious beauty on the head of the valley? Hold on!* I remembered the temple on the hill at the head of the valley. *Who's Ephraim?* I looked it up in the notes. The word meant "fruitful"? Like the Kii Peninsula, smelling of plums, used to make wine and get people drunk. Like Mei's uncle and the guy who'd killed Dr. Dale! I looked up *wreath.* It meant "an entwined crown." In a flash I saw Paul entwining his fingers to explain how religions and traditions

control the culture. *Woe to the fading flower . . . Lotus.* Chills
rolled over me like waves as I read on down, details about
where we'd been and what we'd done in clear detail. He was
speaking to me right from the page! From an ancient book
alive in my hands! I dropped the Bible on my chest and
covered my face with the back of my hand. "Unbelievable!"

A whisper hissed in my ear, "What's wrong?" I jumped.
It was Reece, her eyes sleepy and scared. "Elijah?"

"You gotta hear this!" I sat up and woke the others. In the
warm, windy park I read the verses, explaining as I went.

"'Woe to that wreath, the pride of Ephraim's drunkards.'
It's a warning to the culture that keeps people from
believing in God and to the peninsula that prays to idols
for wine that ruins people's lives. 'To the fading flower, his
glorious beauty, set on the head of a fertile valley—to that
city, the pride of those laid low by wine!' That's Lotus and
his temple on the hill overlooking the valley.

"'See, the Lord has one who is powerful and strong.'"

Dr. Eloise broke in. "Ah yes! Originally this passage
was a warning to Israel around 750 BC that the Assyrians
were attacking. It was God's judgment against Israel, often
called Ephraim because their fruitful valleys were filled with
vineyards. But go on, tell us what it means to you."

"'Like a hailstorm and a destructive wind, like a driving
rain and a flooding downpour, he will throw it forcefully to
the ground.'" Excitedly, I said, "It's like the stream where
we waded, the swift stream from the typhoon that washed

out the road to that old saloon. It repeats the phrase: 'That wreath, the pride of Ephraim's drunkards, will be trampled underfoot. That fading flower, his glorious beauty, set on the head of a fertile valley.' It says this twice; we went to two temples on two hills. It 'will be like a fig ripe before harvest—as soon as someone sees it and takes it in his hand, he swallows it.'"

Rob sat up. "That's like me grabbing up the figs?"

"Yeah, just like you gobbled up the figs, that's how God is going to destroy Lotus. It's our prayer journey, guys, the whole thing here in facts and symbols. Our prayers were an actual war against Lotus, who rules the peninsula, who keeps people lulled senseless by booze, who controls them with the fancy temples built in his honor and the little shrines dedicated to him."

Marcus's green eyes flashed. "You're saying that God knew we'd make this prayer journey almost three thousand years ago?"

"I'm just saying it's written here exactly the way we did it. I stuck my finger in the Bible, and there it was. Here's the rest: 'In that day the LORD Almighty will be a glorious crown, a beautiful wreath for the remnant of his people.'

"That's your little church, Mei, the ones who belong to him no matter what. The left-outs and the leftovers. The remnant. 'He will be a spirit of justice to him who sits in judgment, a source of strength to those who turn back the battle at the gate.'"

I beamed at Reece. "That's you praying at the *torii.*"

Dr. Eloise looked totally lost, so we backed up and went through those days again: how I'd felt a huge darkness going into the peninsula, how Rob gobbled up all the figs, how we swam in the typhoon-swollen stream that had washed out the road to the saloon, how we'd flown into Osaka on the wing of that very typhoon. We told her how the woman's dream of the threatening flower must have meant Lotus, represented in temples carved with useless stone flowers. All of which was just a symbol for what hides beneath it: the beast.

Then, as nice and easy as I could, I told Dr. Eloise about Mei's uncle coming home drunk, how it embarrassed her and bothered the boys. I braced everyone for what happened next: Lotus had spoken through Kenji, demanding I leave. "Now I know why. He didn't want us invading his turf with the sword of the Lord." I held up Reece's Bible. "He saw it coming."

Dr. Eloise stopped me there. "Dear, not to put too fine a point on it, but since we are talking about an entire peninsula here, this Lotus is probably a principality, a high-level arch-demon over a territory. Dear Heaven!"

I explained how I had stood watch and didn't get any sleep. I apologized for being moody and figured that was part of Lotus's evil plan to mess with our spiritual warfare. Lotus had got me so got caught up in thinking about it, I almost forgot to concentrate on God. I realized I'd messed up our *koinonia* over Marcus and Mei, which was none of my business. The evil one had tried every angle to wreck us.

As Reece told her part, I pictured her leading us around the gates with her little hand on the huge posts, commanding those ancient doors to let the Lord in, telling the universe that the king of glory was coming through.

Marcus dropped back against the Elf Tree. "This totally rocks. We were following precise ancient marching orders and didn't know it!"

Dr. Eloise shook her head eerily. "My word, children. I have done many of these journeys in my life and have never seen the likes of this."

Rob grabbed the Bible and read it for himself. "It's a play-by-play, all right. Totally spooky!"

Dr. Eloise said, "You understand why he led you to this chapter, Elijah? The answer is in verse 6. The Lord promised to be a source of supernatural strength to those who fight his battles. Sometimes we do what God says without understanding why until later. It's a walk of faith."

I sank against the Elf Tree beside Marcus. "I messed up."

Dr. Eloise smiled at me. "The entity told you to leave, but you didn't."

"I wanted to."

"But you didn't. We may feel thoroughly out of sorts doing the right thing. One cannot count on feelings."

I looked over my clan, and suddenly every moment with them was as priceless as the red diamonds they wore.

The park was still deserted, the breeze cooler. In three short weeks, we'd fought off typhoon fears, the shock of Dr. Dale's death, bone-aching weariness, dumb spats, and demon threats. Now, in a matter of minutes, everything had changed again. In six little verses, he'd given us back everything we'd lost. No one was tired anymore. I raised my heart to him. *You really are the king of glory, strong and mighty in battle. Your weapons are the words.*

Mei and Marcus bought *bentous*. We hung out in the park like a bunch of regular Japanese kids: Mei and Mayu, Shinobu, Ryo, and me—Takumi. We were lounging around in golden afternoon light and sea breezes. Paradise.

Over noodles and peach nectar, Mei said to Reece and me, "I understand the kind of war we fight with the armor of God and a sword, which is his Word of power. I see it now."

"Yeah, and about your cousin," I said protectively, "I think we need to get you out of there—back to Magdeline."

"I think I've got it." Rob was fiddling with the suitcase of armor pieces to show our mysterious new piece to Dr. Eloise.

"Got what?" I asked.

"There are two bigger rings on that glittery stuff. I think I know why." He'd gotten Mei to pry open the secret compartment, and with the tail of his T-shirt he lifted out the strange mesh. He raised it to eye level. "This goes on the sword," he said.

"How? Where?" I asked.

"I'll show you." He disassembled the sword very carefully.

"How can putting that on get us the word?" Marcus asked him skeptically.

"I don't know, but see these bigger rings at each end, like on a necklace? Well, you can't put it around your neck; it would cut you to shreds. It's too small for a waistband. But hold it this way, and it's the same length as the blade." He fit one loop over the blade tip, stretched the mesh, and then hooked the other loop over the tang, the tab that goes down into the hilt. It was a perfect fit. His fingers bled a little from reassembling the sword. Then he held it up. The piece hung like a ragged flag, limp but sparkling like a waterfall, shaped like flames.

Rob handed it to me. "Try it out."

"Whaddya mean? Try what?"

"I don't know. Just try."

I stood and took the sword handle cautiously with both hands. I drew it back and forth slowly. The others leaned away from it. The piece quivered silkily, glimmered, and sparkled. It was strange and beautiful. I brandished it with easy sweeping movements. When it caught the sun, it almost seemed to disappear, leaving a trail of light.

I brought it up, took a swipe at a small branch of the tree. The sword sliced the branch, the trailing flame shredded the leaves, which fell like confetti on the clan.

Dr. Eloise said powerfully, "'The word of God is living and active. Sharper than any double-edged sword, it penetrates even to dividing soul and spirit, joints and marrow; it judges the thoughts and attitudes of the heart. Nothing in all creation is hidden from God's sight. Everything is uncovered and laid bare before the eyes of him to whom we must give account.'"

It might be my last chance. With only the clan around, I wasn't shy anymore. I put on the whole armor. I moved out to the open lawn of the park, brandishing the sword of the Lord full force with all my might. Back and forth it went, catching the light, becoming light as it sliced the air. Wind whizzed through the mesh and made a sound. Not a *whoosh* like you might think. A strange sound like a human whisper.

I stopped. "Did you hear that?"

Marcus's eyes locked on the blade. "Heard it. Do it again."

Spellbound, the others listened as I swept the sword back and forth through the breeze faster and faster, watching the mesh spiral around the blade like a whirlwind of flame. The sound was always the same, something like *heee-ahhh-ooo-ehhh* but all connected, like a *hyahwheh*. Suddenly Dr. Eloise cried out and clasped her hands to her chest. I stopped.

Mei ran to her. "Oh, are you sick? Is your heart okay?"

Dr. Eloise asked, "Did you not hear it?"

I said, "Yes, but—"

"It speaks the name, children! It speaks *the name!*"

Reece cried, "It's the word, Elijah! Do it again!"

I raised the sword with both hands, unable to breathe for

a moment, eyes locked on the sword, a sheet of fiery light dripping from its blade. I brandished the sword again and again. *Hyahwheh . . . Hyahwheh . . .*

Next thing we knew, we were all hugging and laughing and being all squishy. Beside herself with joy, Dr. Eloise went all teacherly and said, "Children, you remember your vowels from grade school? A, E, I, O, and U. They are the current on which all language flows. Just try to say something and leave out the vowels. Try saying '*bentous* are delicious' without vowels. Go ahead, try." We tried and sounded stupid. "Do you see? Without vowels, no spoken language works. Now here is the beauty of his name: it is formed from the vowels IAOUE, spoken *eeaaoouueh*. Yahweh."

We all tried it.

She repeated, "See, children? The name—his name—is the current on which all language flows. He is the word and he is *in* every word. Please, let us hear it again as it was spoken perhaps from the very Garden of Eden, the name that grants entrance into paradise, or blocks its path forever!"

With the late sun shining, the sea breezes blowing, and my clan watching with pure joy, I whirled across the park like a warrior fighting invisible foes, brandishing the flaming sword of the Lord, listening to it sing his name. I danced and spun in the wind until my arms ached and I was dizzy and drenched in sweat. The verse about the lotus came to me: "*Look at the behemoth. . . . He ranks first among the works of God, yet his Maker can approach him with his sword.*"

Only with the sword of the Lord had we been able to confront Lotus, an alias for the satanic creature concealed in the shadow of temples and statues. As I brandished the sword, I wondered what God had protected us from. *Had Reece been targeted for death on that street in Nikko? Had Dr. Dale taken the hit for her? Should I have drowned among the reeds at the swimming hole, my body washed out to sea downstream at the suicide cliff? What other disasters had God saved us from?* We'd probably never know. Hearing his name fill the air around me, I remembered cursing at him, raging that I wanted nothing to do with him or his sword. My heart hurt. He should have held me under in those stupid reeds or let me get hit by the car and save himself some big trouble. But he didn't. He let me live, let me have his sword; he'd forgiven me and made everything right. Better than right. He'd called me out of my life and into his. Me, Elijah Creek. All I had to do was say okay.

I spun across the lawn—I didn't ever, ever want to stop—and reclaimed the name which he had hidden in *my* name from my birth: *My name is Elijah: El is Yah. My God is Yahweh!*

If the police had come by and seen me—a *henna gaijin* swinging a deadly weapon in a city park—I'd have been arrested for sure.

Chapter 16

WE got our gear together, walked back to the youth hostel, and got our bunkrooms. The hostel was cheap but nice, with crazy decorations in the lobby that were great for a laugh: a stuffed mongoose wrestling a stuffed rattlesnake in a glass case, a foot massage chart, and faded art of zoo animals by a guy named Ivan Itch. We were giddy about everything. We got cleaned up and went out for beef teriyaki. As we waited for the food to come, Reece said, "Guess what! Mei killed a giant centipede in our room. Careepy! But she doesn't believe in reincarnation anymore."

We gave her high fives.

Mei said, "All of a sudden, it didn't make sense to me anymore. I should not kill a spider because it may be my grandmother, but I eat fish and chickens and cows? If reincarnation is true, then we could be eating our grandmothers. But no, I am not a carnival!"

Rob fell off his chair. "*Cannibal*. You're not a cannibal!"

When our meals came, Dr. Eloise said sadly, "After tomorrow we shall not see one another for a long while." Her eyes flickered on me a second before she went back to breaking apart her chopsticks. "If you have issues, let us discuss them."

Issues? We five drew blanks.

"Let me reiterate then: Lotus is—I suspect—a principality. In other parts of Asia, especially in the north, grotesque worship practices involve the lotus. Yes, children, for whatever reason, you have come across a very ancient power and have ruffled his nest to the point that he has manifested." She looked around at us with a kind of worry and awe. "Who *are* you children in the Almighty's eyes? I would love to know. But . . . one must not be so enamored with mysteries that his heart drifts from the Almighty himself."

While we ate, I mentioned how I'd been confused about God's silence during my prayer journey—why he waited until the end to explain things.

"His silence means you are to listen and wait. Twice in history God was silent for an entire epoch: four hundred years of slavery and silence in Egypt followed by an explosion of miracles. And Israel was freed. Four hundred years of silence before Jesus' birth and another explosion of miracles. All of mankind was freed from death." Dr. Eloise looked kindly at Mei. "From the Shimbara Rebellion when most believers were exterminated to the present is nearly four hundred years. Some say God has been silent in Japan. I believe, dear heart, that the silence is ending. When he speaks, there will be both judgment and rescue. There is much work to do and not much time."

"What should I do?" Mei asked earnestly.

"Live your life and grow in your faith. Wear the armor and protect yourself with the Word."

I cleared my throat, "Uh, Dr. E, I was sort of thinking we should get her out of here. Because of . . . Lotus."

"Hmm," Dr. Eloise said thoughtfully. "We shall pray and weigh our options."

Strongly, Mei said, "My little church needs me for now. I will be like Amakusa Shiro. I will not retreat. But I pray that my parents let me visit Magdeline and see my friends."

Dr. Eloise served up tea all around. "Now about your astonishing revelation from Isaiah 28. Highly unusual!"

I said, "I'd already figured that the Quella was three-dimensional."

"Yes, you may find many levels of meaning in one passage. This is an unfathomable mystery, how the living Word of God teaches and reveals to one and all in a billion ways and at any moment at any place on earth. It is a powerful gift! One must take great, great care not to misquote or misinterpret it."

"How can you be sure you're not?" Rob asked.

"By a relationship with the author. When you know him, you'll know what he means. You pray, listen, read, and observe. Discuss your ideas with others; learn from those with more experience. Keep in mind that the evil one knows Scripture too and is adept at twisting it to suit his purpose. One final matter: what shall we do with the armor of God?"

Mei said, "Keep it with Dr. Dale's remains? You wanted to put it in a casket to keep safe."

"I am rethinking that idea." She looked at me.

Marcus said, "One thing's for sure, we can't haul it through airport security more than once. I'm not having my name connected to a string of international incidents."

Through the meal, Reece kept watching me in a strange way. I could hardly look her in the eye. She was reading me like a book. Always could.

Dr. Eloise came pecking on our door late that night. She wanted to talk to me. "Have you decided?" she asked when I'd closed the door behind me.

I didn't know. I'd had this wild idea about tracking the armor across the world, uncovering its history, seeing where it led. But it had been just a dream.

She handed me the suitcase. "Take the armor, Elijah. Find a good hiding place . . . in Magdeline?"

"Well . . . I was thinking that Mei's parents would more likely let her visit the States if they knew the clan had disbanded . . . if the ringleader was gone."

"I see," she smiled.

"But if I'm on the move—if I go with the SOS— there's the problem of getting a sword through security everywhere."

"Ships have safes for the crew's valuables. Wherever you might disembark, your treasure could stay on board. When difficulties arise—and they will—it will remind you. His name must be proclaimed throughout the world."

"You're . . . sure you don't want it?" I asked.

Her small, glittery eyes drilled into me: "Our Mr. Dowland was in error, child. The armor of God must never again rest in peace!"

After a long pause, I said, "Could you help me make an international call?"

She smiled, pulled something metallic out of her pocket, and folded it into my hand. "Follow me."

It shouldn't have been hard for a bunch of teenagers to say good-bye to an old person like Dr. Eloise, who'd always been a little left of center. But we all had a tough time that next morning. We promised to keep in touch.

On the slow train from Shimabara to the seaport, I plugged in Mei's music and watched the rice fields go by. What she said in Ireland was right: there's no other green like rice fields in August—nature's neon. I watched my clan. Rob was asleep on his backpack. Marcus was talking to Mei. Sitting on the opposite side of the train, Reece locked eyes with me in a way that sent my heart into my throat. She'd been watching me awhile. I smiled at her. She smiled back. It seemed like a scene from a movie: blue mountains and sky whizzing past behind her, background music floating through my brain. I was suspended between worlds, between going and staying. I was in Ireland on the Hill of Slane where Marcus had said we were the new wave. Ireland, where I'd first heard about the *peregrini,* the wanderers, where we'd searched for the sword when we had it all along.

But no wild-goose chase there; I'd needed to build Patrick's fire. Like I needed to see the statue of Amakusa Shiro and hear about the carpet of bones, so I'd have the courage to stand against whatever was to come. In that look that passed between Reece and me, we relived it all: a three-year quest from Magdeline to Farr Island to Ireland and beyond.

My whole life is in Magdeline. How can I leave?

It seemed that God had chosen the Magdeline Five to go into all the world and spread his Word. (Actually God meant that call for everyone, but only a few are listening.) To start with, I wouldn't need anything but a transcript of my grades and my parents' permission. Dom had already been talking to them. Mom and Dad had cried on the phone with me the night before. Mom apologized for being a bad mom, and I told her to cut it out. That wasn't the reason I was going. I had to go; it was a God thing. I had all I needed for Samoa: a few changes of clothes, a toothbrush, and the Quella with fresh batteries. Bare necessities.

Mei treated us to the world's best ramen in a little shop on the Hakata station platform. The end of the line. We slurped ourselves silly, ate out the noodles, and lifted our bowls to not miss a drop of the broth.

While Reece and Mei looked at postcards, I bequeathed my weapons to Marcus and Rob: "In my closet are my bow and arrow, a Bowie knife, a few other things. Use them while I'm gone." Rob almost blew a gasket. I figured he sort of already knew. "I'm thinking about going with the SOS. I'm not sure yet." He looked like he was going to cry. Marcus stared down the train tracks, his jaw muscles clamped.

I was their leader. How could I leave?

A bus dropped us off at the harbor. Huge—and I mean huge—car ferries were backed up to pier ramps so that cars could drive into the lower level.

Mei pointed up to a row of windows near the top deck. "We stay up there." She took care of business at the counter, then led us up a fancy winding staircase with gold rails to a big room lined with mats and pillows. "Family room," she apologized. "The sleeping is not too comfortable for you, I think. But food and the *ofuro* on ferries are very good."

The ship set out. The wind picked up, and I started feeling what life might be like for me. Open sea. Survival training. Adventures. Danger. Taking the armor of God around the world. No family, no home, no Camp Mudj. No clan. No Reece.

I was ripped in two.

The cafeteria was packed. We laughed and chitchatted like old times, but everyone had a kind of scared sadness behind their eyes. My heart was in a big knot. I couldn't think about climbing Great Oak with Rob in summer. Or driving the golf cart through Owl Woods with Reece when yellow leaves fall like flakes of light. I wouldn't be running into the house smelling like campfire and have the twins jump on me and Mom take care of me like she used to. I wouldn't be working with Dad or hanging out at Florence's.

Mei wrote a *kanji* symbol on her napkin and gave it to Rob. "This is ninja. It is made of three symbols: sword, heart, and person. The sword and heart together mean either 'hidden' or 'endure.' So," she sniffled, "we are all ninja. We hide or we endure, for the sake of the sword."

Reece looked out the window at the sea, "We hide the sword in our hearts."

She was on deck watching the sun go down, her hair blowing in the wind, the big ship engines roaring underneath the deck. I came up beside her and saw tears running down her cheeks.

"This is way cool, huh?" I said stupidly.

She nodded and there was a strangely unnerving expression on her face. A lump formed in my gut. "Reece?"

"Elijah, I'm letting you go."

I knew what she meant, but then I didn't. "What do you mean?" I asked.

"I'm letting you go, as simple as that."

I waited for more.

"That's your destiny, out there with the Students of the Seven Seas."

"It only lasts two years. Then I'll graduate. I'll be back."

Her head shook fiercely. "You're meant to go into all the world. It's your calling to trace the path of the armor.

Everything's falling into place—" her words caught in her throat, "just like I planned."

"You can go with me. We can all go, as soon as there's an opening. Hey, remember what I always said: if I'm going, you're going. I said it on Devil's Cranium. And when we went to Ireland. And coming here to Japan. And . . . and out there too." I nodded to the sunset making red streaks across dark water.

"Not this time."

"Reece . . ."

"I'd just hold you back."

"No, you won't. You're the reason I'm here. Who knows where I'd be if you hadn't . . . if you hadn't prayed?"

"You'll be going into dangerous places where you should travel incognito. American girls on crutches stick out like sore thumbs."

"You'll get more surgeries."

She turned to me with conviction. "It won't help."

"You don't know that."

"Yes, I do." She turned back resolutely to the red sky. She was scaring me.

"What are you talking about?"

"It's settled between God and me."

"If you know something, you can't leave me out of the loop," I tried to joke. "It's my life."

"Yes. It is."

I spun her around. "What's settled? You have to tell me."

She bit her lip to stop it from trembling. "When . . . when you got hurt in Gilead, and the doctors considered amputating your foot, that day I prayed for God to work a miracle, like he did for me that night I was in the hospital and in so much pain." She cried, "They were talking about cutting off your foot!"

A terrible feeling welled up in me. "What did you do?"

"I made a deal . . . with God. I prayed for him to take what was wrong with you and give it to me. That if you were never to walk again, that it would be me instead."

"What are you talking about? The doctor said the frostbite wasn't that bad."

"That was later. Things changed . . . after I prayed. You got better."

"In another couple of years, doctors will have new technology."

She shook her head. "It's settled, Elijah. You're the Magdelinian."

"What's that mean, Reece? I don't even know what that means!"

"I think it just means that God has had his eye on you from the first. That he brought you to this place and time for his purpose. He's given you the ancestry of the first Magdelinians, made you to know the Indian ways to survive, let your mom be adopted from the Isle of Magdeline so you could live free in Magdeline, Ohio. And now you're like Mary Magdalene because you're fighting off demons and following Jesus. It's how he does things, bringing all the details together across time and space. Like he did with us and Isaiah 28. It's his way of showing us he knows what he's doing and that we should pay attention."

"Why should God answer your prayers and not mine?" I huffed. "I'm the head of this operation."

She just shook her head, her lips trembling. "He . . . told me." She looked out at the sea and with her strong Scripture voice said, "'A voice of one calling in the desert, "Prepare the way for the Lord, make straight paths for him."' That was written about the second Elijah and maybe the third too. 'Pass through the gates! Prepare the way for the people.'"

The past three years spread out . . . me climbing through the broken basement window of Old Pilgrim Church; that moment when Reece held the helmet for the first time, all aglow in my campfire, a look of mystery in her eyes; her bringing Marcus into the clan against my objections; how she supported me all through the trouble about the Kate Dowland mystery, saying, "If anyone can solve it, you can." Reece calling me at Farr Island to tell me she had Dowland's journals, telling me to hurry back. The tornado, how we all clung together in the dark while God tore through The Castle, his backhanded way of putting Rob's family back together and uncovering the truth in that closet about the MacMerrits. Which had led us to Ireland. Which had traced my roots as a Magdelinian back to the dawn of history. I pictured Reece and Rob in their silly green elf outfits at the

Christmas Village. I remembered playing the eagle-bone whistle on a frosty night in Owl Woods. It was Reece's gift to me so I could play songs to God.

Her prayer had helped Mei and Rob decode the breastplate. It was her courage and faith that kept me calm when she went down at Hermits' Cave. Her prayers gave me peace when I was trapped in Gilead. If it hadn't been for Reece Elliston pressing the authorities to sweep Telanoo at night to look for me, I'd be a pile of bones in Gilead.

I remembered how on the plane to Ireland she was willing to give me up if I liked Emma. "I want us to always be friends," she'd said. And when Mom and Dad weren't excited about my baptism, Reece had squeezed my hand and told me I had courage. I'd circled the planet, and I was wearing the armor of God because of her. Without Reece showing me God, I'd have stayed at Camp Mudj and had a real nice ordinary life.

Her voice broke into my thoughts. "Mei named you Takumi—explore the ocean—even before she knew! You should run free, Elijah—it's what you love."

"I know . . . but . . . it's not the only thing I love."

Sometime around midnight Rob came on deck to look for us. Reece was asleep and wrapped in a blanket in her deck chair, her head on my shoulder, her hand in mine. Rob crossed the deck, hands in his pockets, arms stiff against the brisk wind. His eyebrows went up when he saw my drained expression. He slowed, stopped, and stood frowning at us, the wind whipping his jacket. I gave him a look and shook my head, which meant *dokka ike!* Shrugging, a little embarrassed, he left. I reminded myself to give him my samurai kite to take to Nori and Stacy.

God had pulled me into his bow, stretched me to the breaking point, and then released. *I'm going*, I said, amazed. *All I'm asking is one thing. Why can't you heal her?*

The sky was so black and clear the stars didn't even twinkle.

As the early sky brightened, I looked up *leave home* in the Quella to see if God had anything to say about it. "No one who has left home or wife or brothers or parents or children for the sake of the kingdom of God will fail to receive many times as much in this age and, in the age to come, eternal life."

I know, God, but what about your verse saying that a cord of five strands is not quickly broken? Yeah, it actually says three strands, but you know what I mean. We five were supposed to stay together, the Magdeline Five! Does one verse cancel out another?

My Word is true.

I sat staring into the night. Never—not in my wildest dreams—did I ever imagine that an innocent peek into an old church would change my life forever, turning me into the wild vagabond that I am now. But it did.

Over the sound of waves and ship engines he called me, *Elijah. . . .*

I'm here, I answered. The wind whirled around me. A thin

string of lights twinkled from a distant island shore. In a few hours we'd be in Osaka port. Mei would take the others to the airport. I'd wait at the dock for the SOS ship. I was alone, and I guessed that's how it would be. My mission, I figured, was somehow to prepare the people for the war to come. I'd have to stay on the move to get the word out, my piece of the Tear of Blood stapled to my belly, the armor and sword in my keeping. I'd have to keep the last bit of advice Dr. Eloise had whispered in my ear: "Steer clear of treasure hunters." She probably meant that Cravens and his kind wouldn't give up. Some people would never get it about the real armor of God: the *omen* truth which sets things right; righteousness to protect your heart; faith in unseen powers to ward off the evil one's fiery arrows (like whatever demons would be slithering out from behind the veil next); unexplainable peace; salvation and hope no matter what; the flaming sword as powerful as any weapon devised, for storming the gates of Hell.

I pulled out the medallion on the chain around my neck—the metallic thing Dr. Eloise had slipped into my hand. I ran my fingers over it, feeling the strands of the three coils: migration. God's command given three times to the world: go, go, go fill the earth with my goodness.

I'm going.

Elijah . . .

I'm here, Master of Breath.

Take heart. A cord of five strands is not quickly broken.

Author's Note

※※※

MY greatest adventures and deepest friendships are rooted in Japan, one of the safest, most progressive countries in The Window. However, it remains the stronghold of millions of gods, of principalities and powers.

The events related to the prayer journey at the Nikko shrine and on the Kii Peninsula, including the encounter with a lotus principality, are based on actual events in the summers of 2002 and 2004. The actual spiritual preparation for those trips was far more strenuous than described in the book. And unknown to our team at the time, the prayer journey to Kii was described in startling detail in Isaiah 28!

The actual full armor of God is made real for its wearer through faith in the life, death, and resurrection of Jesus, the Word: the sword.

Your armor is ready. Put it on!

· ·

Read more about the Elijah Creek characters,
the armor of God,
and spiritual warfare at:

www.lenawood.com

Ancient Truth

※※

(Page 21) "He gave them power and authority to drive out all demons and to cure diseases, and he sent them out. . . . He told them: 'Take nothing for the journey—no staff, no bag, no bread, no money, no extra tunic.'"

Luke 9:1-3

(Page 31, 70) "Lift up your heads, O you gates; be lifted up, you ancient doors, that the King of glory may come in. Who is this King of glory? The LORD strong and mighty, the LORD mighty in battle. . . . He is the King of glory."

Psalm 24:7-10

(Page 57) "As the deer pants for streams of water, so my soul pants for you, O God. My soul thirsts for God, for the living God. When can I go and meet with God?"

Psalm 42:1, 2

(Page 62) "In the beginning was the Word, and the Word was with God, and the Word was God."

John 1:1

(Page 64) ". . . and the sword of the Spirit, which is the word of God. And pray in the Spirit on all occasions with all kinds of prayers and requests."

Ephesians 6:17, 18

(Page 65, 139) "Our struggle is not against flesh and blood, but . . . against the powers of this dark world and against the spiritual forces

of evil in the heavenly realms. Therefore put on the full armor of God."

Ephesians 6:12

(Page 68) "I am the LORD your God. . . . You shall have no other gods before me."

Exodus 20:2, 3

(Page 70) "This is what the LORD says to you: 'Do not be afraid or discouraged because of this vast army. For the battle is not yours, but God's.'"

2 Chronicles 20:15

(Page 70, 168) "The word of God is living and active. Sharper than any double-edged sword, it penetrates even to dividing soul and spirit, joints and marrow; it judges the thoughts and attitudes of the heart. Nothing in all creation is hidden from God's sight. Everything is uncovered and laid bare before the eyes of him to whom we must give account."

Hebrews 4:12, 13

(Page 70, 149) "This is the gate of the LORD through which the righteous may enter."

Psalm 118:20

(Page 71) "The poor and needy search for water, but there is none; their tongues are parched with thirst. But I the LORD will answer them; I, the God of Israel, will not forsake them."

Isaiah 41:17

(Page 73) "To the arrogant I say, 'Boast no more,' and to the wicked, 'Do not lift up your horns. Do not lift your horns against heaven; do

not speak with outstretched neck.' No one from the east or the west or from the desert can exalt a man. But it is God who judges."

Psalm 75:4-7

(Page 74, 182) "Pass through, pass through the gates! Prepare the way for the people. Build up, build up the highway! Remove the stones."

Isaiah 62:10

(Page 77) ". . . a holy nation, a people belonging to God, that you may declare the praises of him who called you out of darkness into his wonderful light. Once you were not a people, but now you are the people of God."

1 Peter 2:9, 10

(Page 89) "The Almighty will be your gold, the choicest silver for you. Surely then you will find delight in the Almighty and will lift up your face to God. You will pray to him, and he will hear you, and you will fulfill your vows. What you decide on will be done, and light will shine on your ways."

Job 22:25-28

(Page 91) "I praise you, Father, Lord of heaven and earth, because you have hidden these things from the wise and learned, and revealed them to little children."

Matthew 11:25

(Page 91) "The price of wisdom is beyond rubies."

Job 28:18

(Page 108) Humble yourselves before the Lord, and he will lift you up."

James 4:10

(Page 119) "Go and make disciples of all nations."

Matthew 28:18

(Page 128, 145) "Under the lotus plants he lies, hidden among the reeds in the marsh. The lotuses conceal him in their shadow."

Job 40:21

(Page 128, 170) "Look at the behemoth. . . . He ranks first among the works of God, yet his Maker can approach him with his sword."

Job 40:15-19

(Page 138) "Satan . . . leads the whole world astray." "The prince of this world now stands condemned."

Revelation 12:9; John 16:11

(Page 142) "I am the light of the world. Whoever follows me will never walk in darkness, but will have the light of life."

John 8:12

(Page 143) "Faith is being . . . certain of what we do not see."

Hebrews 11:1

(Page 158) "[Ezekiel] saw a great many bones on the floor of the valley, bones that were very dry. [The Lord] asked . . . , 'Can these bones live?'"

Ezekiel 37:2, 3

(Page 158) "[The martyrs] called out in a loud voice, 'How long, Sovereign Lord, holy and true, until you judge the inhabitants of the earth and avenge our blood?' Then each of them was given a white robe, and they were told to wait a little longer, until the number of their fellow servants and brothers who were to be killed as they had been was completed."

Revelation 6:10, 11

(Page 162–164) "Woe to that wreath, the pride of Ephraim's drunkards, to the fading flower, his glorious beauty, set on the head of a fertile valley—to that city, the pride of those laid low by wine! See, the Lord has one who is powerful and strong. Like a hailstorm and a destructive wind, like a driving rain and a flooding downpour, he will throw it forcefully to the ground. That wreath, the pride of Ephraims's drunkards, will be trampled underfoot. That fading flower, his glorious beauty, set on the head of a fertile valley, will be like a fig ripe before harvest—as soon as someone sees it and takes it in his hand, he swallows it. In that day the LORD Almighty will be a glorious crown, a beautiful wreath for the remnant of his people. He will be a spirit of justice to him who sits in judgment, a source of strength to those who turn back the battle at the gate.

Isaiah 28:1-6

(Page 182) "This is he who was spoken of through the prophet Isaiah: 'A voice of one calling in the desert, "Prepare the way for the Lord, make straight paths for him."'"

Matthew 3:3

(Page 184) "No one who has left home or wife or brothers or parents or children for the sake of the kingdom of God will fail to receive many times as much in this age and, in the age to come, eternal life."

Luke 18:29, 30

(Page 184) "A cord of three strands is not quickly broken."

Ecclesiastes 4:12

Creek Code

German
luftkrankheit—(looft-krahnk-heit) Air sickness

Japanese
Mata atode—(mah-tah ah-toh-deh) See you later
Torii—(toh-ree-ee) Shinto gateway to the gods
Onigiri—(oh-nee-ghee-ree) Rice balls with something inside
Ryokan—(ryoh-khan) Japanese-style inn
Ofuro—(oh-foo-roh) Japanese bath
Yukata—(you-kah-tah) Lightweight kimono-style robe
Bentou—(ben-toh) Box lunch
Henna gaijin—(hen-nah gah-ee-jeen) Strange foreigner
Okonomiyaki—(oh-koh-noh-mee-yah-kee) Pancake-like food filled
    with meat and vegetables
Moukari makka—(moh-kah-ree mak-kah) How's business?
Bochibochi denna—(boh-chee-boh-chee den-nah) So-so
Ohayou—(oh-hah-yoh) Good morning
Ume—(oo-meh) Plum
Dokka ike—(doke-kah ee-keh) Get lost!
Fumie—(foo-mee-eh) Picture [of Jesus] to be stepped on

Hebrew
Yahweh—Jehovah, the Lord

Greek
Parabolani—The riskers